Berta La Larga

Cuca Canals was born in 1962 in Barcelona. She worked with Bigas Luna on the film scripts for *Jamón Jamón* and *The Tit and the Moon*, both prize winners at the Venice Film Festival. *Berta La Larga* is her first novel.

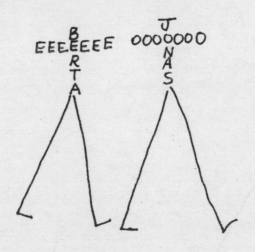

Arga

BERTA LA LARGA

A passionate chronicle
ironical
meteorological
and not very logical

B

R

a

Arga

BERTA LA LARGA

Cuca Canals

Translated from the Spanish by Sonia Soto

⚓ *Anchor*

TRANSWORLD PUBLISHERS LTD
61–63 Uxbridge Road, London W5 5SA

TRANSWORLD PUBLISHERS (AUSTRALIA) PTY LTD
15–25 Helles Avenue, Moorebank, NSW 2170

TRANSWORLD PUBLISHERS (NZ) LTD
3 William Pickering Drive, Albany, Auckland

Published by Anchor – a division of Transworld Publishers Ltd.

First published in Great Britain by Anchor, 1998

Originally published in Spanish by Plaza & Janes, 1996

A catalogue record for this book is available from the British Library.

ISBN 1862 30021 6

Typeset in 11/14pt Adobe Caslon by Phoenix Typesetting, West Yorkshire.
Printed in Great Britain by Mackays of Chatham Plc, Chatham, Kent.

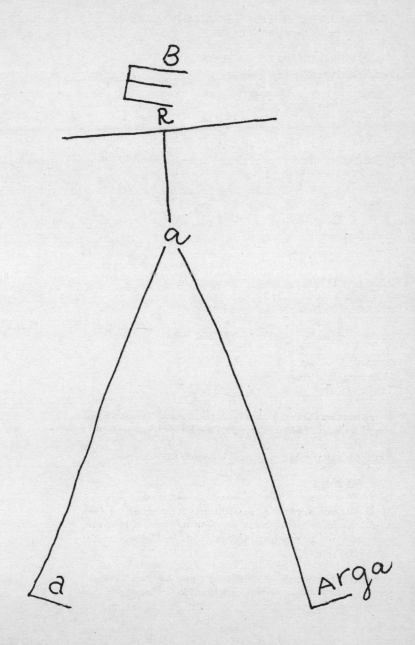

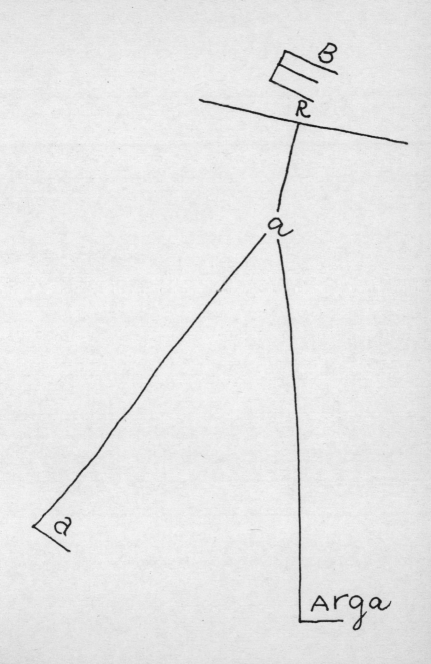

For my parents

Federico the donkey welcomes you to the village of Navidad

Berta Quintana had just turned sixteen. She measured six feet two inches and she was the tallest human being in Navidad and possibly in the entire region. The tallest men there rarely reached five feet five and the women were considered tall if they got to five feet two.

Berta was also very thin and that made her look even taller. She had a fragile beauty – a face that was always pale, very smooth skin, and a timid look in her eyes. Berta hated her height, because it was well known that no man in Navidad wanted a woman so tall that she could look over his shoulder. So she was the only young girl in Navidad who had never known love. Because of this, and also because she was at a very difficult age, she'd wished more than once that she'd never been born. But she had.

*   *   *

On the day that Berta Quintana came into the world it poured with rain. The night before, her father, Juan Quintana, went to fetch the doctor who lived in the village of Ponsa. They reached Navidad at dawn, soaked to the skin and covered in mud. You could hear the cries of pain of the mother-to-be from the street. The doctor was exhausted before he even started. It had been quite an effort just getting to Navidad, and first he wanted to wash from head to foot, not just for the sake of hygiene but also because he was rather vain. Still, the only sign that Berta's birth would be different from any other baby's was that, as labour commenced, the sky cleared and a beautiful Rainbow appeared. The inhabitants of Navidad went into the street and stared open-mouthed at it.

According to an ancient legend in Navidad, a baby born under the Rainbow had special powers. So, in a few seconds, all the villagers had gathered outside the Quintanas' house, as they wanted to know whether the baby was going to come into the world at that precise moment. Even Alberto the Baker, who was very unsociable, stopped his work and came to witness what was believed to be the most important event in the history of the village. The mother, Roberta Anaya, paid more attention to what was going on outside her window than to the doctor's instructions. The excitement was certainly justified. Berta would be the first baby in three hundred years to be born in Navidad under the Rainbow.

All those years of waiting meant that the inhabitants of Navidad, generations and generations of them, had had plenty of opportunity to imagine all kinds of marvels, mostly related to wealth, something they were entirely unfamiliar with. The Rainbow baby was said to be able to turn bread into gold and, with a mere flick of the finger, till the soil, milk a dozen cows at the same time, cut down a whole forest and transform raindrops into coins and bank notes. Some of the villagers, on the other hand, would have been quite content for the Rainbow baby simply to make the village of Ponsa, with which they were on very bad terms, disappear.

As well as these generic powers, the inhabitants of the village congregating outside Juan Quintana's house dreamed that the luck of the Rainbow would be the remedy for their own personal problems. Pedro the Blind Man said he would settle for regaining his sight; married women wanted to be more attractive and slimmer – there was general agreement among husbands on this point, because shortly after getting married their wives became as fat as cows. Alberto the Baker and his wife, Remedios, hoped that their son could be made a bit less simple, because he was born dim-witted. All the kids had fun imagining the toys the Rainbow would bring them and how they'd never have to go to school again: it'd be brilliant. The old people dreamed of being young again, and the smallest children of turning into grown-ups. Women of marriageable age dreamed of their Prince Charming.

Margarita Cifuentes showed the least restraint and wouldn't stop listing wishes: she wanted blue eyes like her great-aunt Margarita, a porcelain complexion like her cousin in the capital, a black servant, a husband with better manners, etc. Others were more modest: one young villager who was completely bald said he'd just like to have hair again. His brother, on the other hand, was already quite hairy, so he just wanted enough money to get on a boat and sail around the world. An old maid with a bit of a complex about being flat-chested dreamed of having voluptuous breasts like Roberta Anaya's, so she could get a man. And even though they'd never admit it, quite a few men dreamed of increased virility. And there was one wish on which they were all agreed: if only the Rainbow could get that pain in the arse Margarita Cifuentes to shut up. She was still banging on: I wish there was a tearoom in Navidad, I wish I had the latest Paris fashions, I wish my husband Feliciano wouldn't burp so loudly, etc.

The only person in Navidad not thinking about the Rainbow was Juan Quintana, the father. He was more concerned about the health of the baby than some meteorological phenomenon, especially when he thought about how dim-witted Alberto the Baker's son had turned out. As he waited outside on the landing, Juan Quintana couldn't stop thinking about his friend, and he felt more and more sorry for him. When Alberto the Baker found out that his son had turned out stupid, he decided not to give him his own name, so he called him Amadeo, which also begins with A. And since then Alberto the Baker had spent each day working from dawn until well after dusk. It meant he didn't have to deal with anyone, or, in particular, think about what a half-wit his son was. Juan Quintana understood now how a man whose job was making sweet things could be so sour. Poor Alberto, and poor Remedios, his wife. Amadeo the Idiot had just turned three and he still couldn't say a single word, and as a baby he could never find his mother's nipple even though he had a good appetite. You couldn't even give him any toys, because he put everything in his mouth, thinking it was food, what a useless son. And Juan Quintana couldn't stand it any longer: 'Why is that doctor taking so long to give me any news?'

If, as they say, good things come to all who wait, this baby was going to have amazing powers, because the labour seemed endless. The doctor took ages to pull the baby out, as if she just went on for ever, especially her legs; and the umbilical cord was so long it could have been used to tie up several undesirables, including that pain in the arse Margarita Cifuentes, and to gag her too, if only. From the room of the mother-to-be, the doctor could hear Margarita Cifuentes and all the others clamouring to know how the baby was, and asking him to hurry up, the

Rainbow wouldn't last for ever, you know. They fetched the priest, who had a direct line to God, and got him to ask for the damn baby to be born once and for all, and the priest did as he was told, on condition that they all came to church for the next year without grumbling. Yes, yes, anything, as long as the Rainbow didn't go away. When they saw how long the labour was lasting, they were gripped with fear: what if the Rainbow disappeared with the baby only half out? They pondered the question, until somebody said that in that case they would only be granted half a wish. For instance, if the Rainbow had decided to present them with gold, they'd get silver instead, and if it granted them their wish of no longer having to work, then they'd have to work half days, and Pedro the Blind Man would only see out of one eye, and the women would only become a year or two younger. The young man who dreamed of sailing across the sea saw his boat run out of steam in the middle of the ocean and sink. The bald man would only get half a head of hair, and that would make things even worse. But the old maid was the most anxious, what if only one of her breasts grew and the other one remained just as flat, she'd be a monster. So they came to the conclusion that it would be best if Berta was born quickly, and again they asked the doctor to hurry, and they all knelt in the street to pray with the priest. At first, the doctor had enjoyed having such a large audience, but now it was making him nervous and he leaned out of the window and asked them to pray quietly: 'God isn't deaf you know.' But first he combed his hair to make himself more presentable. Juan Quintana had to go outside twice to ask his neighbours to be quiet and let the doctor get on with his work, and he finally handed his friend Joseph the Carpenter the key to the tavern so he could let them all in and serve them drinks on his, Juan Quintana's, behalf – they'd have to pay for them of course, he had an extra mouth to feed now, he couldn't very well be expected to offer them on the house, now could he?

When the doctor at last saw the child in her entirety he fell silent, because he'd never seen such a huge baby before. He needed fifteen cloths to clean her up, and three more to mop the sweat from his forehead, and then he wrapped her in a towel, but it was too small, he simply couldn't get it to cover her legs. Afterwards he showed her to her mother, Roberta Anaya, who was so exhausted she just kept repeating, 'Rainbow, Rainbow,' over and over again, and the doctor, who didn't know about the legend, thought: That's a strange name for a little girl.

As Juan Quintana still hadn't heard anything from the doctor, he thought his daughter must have come out faulty. Only after the doctor had had a whisky and recovered the power of speech did Juan Quintana find out that the child, though long, was normal, and then he had to have a whisky himself to get over the terrible fright he'd given himself. The doctor wanted to charge double for his services – what with the child being so long, he'd had extraordinary difficulty getting her out. Juan Quintana took offence and not only paid him strictly the normal fee but also deducted the price of the whisky.

Leaving the house, the doctor was pounced on by the villagers, as they all wanted to know what special gift the child had. When they found out that it was just that she was un-usually long, there was general disappointment. All that waiting and for what, for a baby that was as long as a salami. Juan Quintana wasn't too pleased by the look of despair on his neighbour's faces, and to defend his daughter's dignity, he concocted his own theory as to why she was so long. He stated with great confidence that it was due to Roberta Anaya's putting too much yeast in the bread on one occasion during the pregnancy, and this meant that the baby had grown bigger than was usual in the mother's belly. He also said that perhaps his daughter's special gift would manifest itself over time, but nobody listened.

They all went home, heads bowed, except for the priest who'd made them promise that they'd go to church every Sunday for the next year without grumbling. Juan Quintana had to console his wife. Roberta Anaya was also disappointed that the child was so long, particularly as she'd knitted several woollies and pairs of booties and embroidered some shirts, and now she was sure they wouldn't fit.

Juan Quintana picked up his daughter and smiled happily. He thought he was the luckiest father in the world. He looked out of the window at the Rainbow and thanked it for giving him a healthy daughter. But, just in case, he took her little finger and touched the window frame with it, to see if it turned to gold. You didn't lose anything by trying.

And the Rainbow disappeared.

The legend of the Rainbow was born over three hundred years ago, when the first settlers arrived in what was later to become known as Navidad. They had searched for a place to live for a long time, and they were now utterly exhausted, because on top of having to carry all their possessions, they'd had to endure the rain, which hadn't abated for several weeks. The moment it stopped raining at last, the Rainbow appeared. One of them said it was a sign from God that this was the chosen place. And the Rainbow waited for them to stand beneath it before disappearing. As it was the twenty-fourth of December, they called the place Navidad and they decided to celebrate the birth of Christ and the village at the same time by building a nativity scene. Using the clay that was everywhere because of all the rain, first they made a Joseph and then a Virgin Mary, proving themselves to be abysmal artists: the figures were so bad that more than one villager considered atheism on seeing them. You really had to use your imagination to recognize them, they were hunchbacks, with grotesquely big heads, a real fright, so, out of respect, they decided they wouldn't make a baby Jesus, son of God. But to their surprise, the following morning, they found a baby made of clay lying in the manger. He was so beautiful that he obviously wasn't the work of humans, or at least not of these particular humans, and there weren't any others for miles around. And while they wondered where he could have come from, the Rainbow appeared again, for no reason whatsoever since the sky was completely clear.

Since then, they'd believed that all children born under the Rainbow, like the clay baby, would have a special gift. They also thought that the Rainbow's magic powers would turn Navidad into an important town. How wrong they were: three centuries later, Navidad was hardly more than a single street lined with flimsy, old wooden houses, covered in ageing layers of paint which did nothing for them, like old women trying to look twenty years younger by plastering on make-up. And Navidad only appeared on local maps, if it appeared at all, with its name printed in tiny letters, as if someone were trying to humiliate them.

Navidad had become a worn-out, godforsaken place, sleepy, aimless. Its major claim to fame was poverty, and although the surrounding countryside was pretty, it was nothing special because the rest of the region was very attractive too. There was nothing in its history to make the inhabitants feel proud. Navidad had no famous sons, no produce worthy of mention, no local crafts. It hadn't even had the misfortune to witness any wars. Nor was it on the way to anywhere, since the road ended there, and as somebody once said, it was like arriving at the end of the earth. Navidad didn't even live up to its name: it had never snowed there, a fact which occasionally made it the object of mockery, particularly by the inhabitants of the neighbouring village of Ponsa. True, Navidad did have its very own legend, but now that a child had at last been born under the Rainbow, it turned out that her only talent was for being very tall. So they preferred to keep quiet about it.

Even the church clock didn't work. Thirty years ago it had stopped at ten past seven, because two inquisitive children playing up in the tower looked inside to see what it was like and broke one of the cogs. For poking about where he shouldn't have, one of the boys almost lost his left hand, and his right hand too – but that was because his father, a very strict man, wanted to teach him a lesson and struck his hand with such ferocity that it was permanently damaged. That was how both time and the child came to be disabled. Those who were forced to go to church were delighted about the clock stopping because now they had an excuse for arriving late.

It seemed as if time, like the church clock, had stopped in Navidad. The mountains contributed to this feeling. They surrounded the village, like parents who protect their children and don't want them to grow up because they fear losing them. On the rare occasions they went to the capital, the villagers were fascinated by the enormous buildings, the cars, the streets full of life, and they were baffled by all the bustle, the mass of humanity, the anonymity of its inhabitants, the honking of horns, the smoke, and they felt disconcerted, just like children who've lost sight of their parents and don't know what to do.

Berta Quintana's family was one of the oldest in Navidad. They had lived there for more than ten generations. Her ancestors were farmers and would still have been farmers had it not been for the accident that befell Berta's great-grandfather. He had a very forceful personality and when he was angry he kicked the door of his room with such fury that, very often, he broke it down and made the whole house shake. This is exactly what happened the year great-grandfather lost his entire harvest because of a plague of insects that arrived the day before he was due to gather in the crops. Unfortunately, when he broke the door down this time he got a splinter in his foot, and the foot became infected, and because they tried to save the foot gangrene spread to his leg and they had to cut if off in such haste that great-grand-mother didn't even have time to recite a rosary.

And great-grandfather's leg, or lack of it, changed the destiny of the Quintana family. Despite the loss of his leg, he still had a family to feed – three children and another one on the way – so he decided to open a tavern. He probably had the idea because he liked drinking so much: he thought fondly of the Don Quixote tavern in the capital. Every time he went there to sell his harvest he paid the Don Quixote a visit. If he got a good price for his crops, he had three brandies, which only happened once, as his crops were nearly always of poor quality, so when he got a bad price he had three brandies to drown his sorrows.

The was how great-grandfather Quintana, following his unfortunate accident, came to invest the little money he had in the purchase of a wooden leg and in constructing the first hostelry in Navidad, and on the second floor he installed his family, since he'd had to sell the farm with its acre of land in order to open the tavern and buy a wooden leg. And from then on, whenever he lost his temper, he no longer kicked things, just in case he lost the other leg, and instead he had a brandy to calm himself down and then he'd find any excuse to have another one. In fact if he was very angry he had three brandies, and even if he wasn't he had three brandies – he was the landlord after all.

The tavern was called The Pirate, which was what great-grandfather thought he looked like with his wooden leg – he might have lost a leg, but he hadn't lost his sense of humour. He asked his wife, Berta's great-grandmother, not to bury his wooden leg with him when he died but to put it at the door to the tavern, under a small sign bearing the name of the establishment. And she did just that when great-grandfather kicked the bucket with his one remaining leg – one fine day his heart just stopped beating. News of his death caused some surprise: people couldn't believe that a man with such a busy life could die so peacefully. That day it was great-grandmother Quintana who downed three brandies, and then she recited a rosary for her husband's soul. She was still young when she was widowed, poor thing, she could have re-married as she was very beautiful, but who could even think about another man with great-grandfather's wooden leg leaning there.

Over forty years had passed since great-grandfather's death but it seemed like yesterday, and now it was Berta's father, Juan Quintana, who ran The Pirate tavern, seeing as he was the only one of his descendants to have remained in Navidad. The others had moved to the capital in search of a new life, and they were heard from no more. The tavern was almost exactly as great-grandfather had left it, except there was a fridge and a cooker, as they now served food together with alcoholic beverages and soft drinks, as well as receiving the post for the entire village, and great-grandfather's leg was still there by the door which was a miracle because twice now it had almost met its end. The first time because of a woodworm infestation in the village, and the second when a cripple, who had no left leg, tried to steal it, but luckily Juan Quintana spotted him. The cripple begged him for it, claiming he didn't have the money to buy himself one. Having a way with words the cripple almost convinced Juan Quintana, but as he soughed and sighed melo-dramatically during his sob-story, Juan Quintana saw that he had two gold teeth, worth a fortune. Juan Quintana snatched the leg away and, furious, bashed the cripple on the head with it in great-grandfather's name and kicked him up the arse, and booted him out of the tavern, in the most literal sense of the term.

Berta's parents married very young. At the time, Roberta Anaya's family lived on a farm on the outskirts of the village: there were five children, twenty hens, three pigs and two cows, and it was Roberta's job to take fresh milk to the village every morning. Juan Quintana only noticed her when she became a woman and, almost from one day to the next, grew two enor-mous breasts: they were so large they were like mountains, and Juan Quintana fell in love with them, although he told her he'd fallen in love with her eyes, thinking as he did so that she would be a perfect mother to the many children he wanted. With breasts like that she could feed an army.

When they became engaged, they went to the lovers' tree, on the outskirts of the village, as was the custom, and carved their names in the trunk. They were to be married very quickly, as Juan Quintana was impatient to taste Roberta's breasts, and being a very respectable young woman she'd told him she'd only allow it after the wedding. The following day Juan Quintana went to talk to Roberta Anaya's parents, and just before entering the house he saw his future wife milking a cow. Juan Quintana licked his lips when he saw that the cow's udders were as large as his fiancée's, and when he saw her mother, he thought Roberta more like the cow, but that wasn't a bad thing, because her mother was the embodiment of ugliness and didn't even have large breasts like her daughter.

They were married a week later in the village church, and the wedding took place in such haste that many thought Roberta must be pregnant. After the ceremony, Juan Quintana tasted Roberta's breasts and liked the left one much more than the right. Although smaller it was sweeter, and ever since, instead of dessert, he sucked her left breast, and did so with such diligence that it really hurt. It was a full year before she dared tell her husband, and then they decided that he would only suck her left breast on Sundays and holidays. On other days her husband had to make do with the right breast, which, being larger, was less sensitive. Roberta turned out to be the perfect wife for Juan Quintana: docile, hard-working, obedient, she said yes to everything, and she never raised her voice, and she made the best bread in Navidad. His only disappointment was that she gave him only one daughter, Berta. And he, who had always wanted lots of children, couldn't understand why God had given Roberta Anaya such large breasts. And he thought that if the Rainbow really had had magic powers the least it could have done was give him quintuplets.

★ *The thing most closely resembling Roberta Anaya's*
left breast

By the age of seven, Berta was already as tall as her mother, and at nine, she was as tall as her father – more than once Juan Quintana had to listen to some unfortunate remark concerning his daughter's height. Although he was a man who didn't often lose his temper, he would leave them in no doubt: 'If I ever hear you say anything about my daughter again, you can get out of my tavern.' Juan Quintana was obsessed with attracting customers, but his daughter was more important: 'She's the only one I have.'

It was around that time that the other children started calling her Berta La Larga. They made fun of her, and didn't want her on their team in games because, being so tall, she was clumsy, and she got nervous and that made things even worse. They said that, because she was so tall, one day the wind would blow her away, like the leaves of the trees, and that frightened Berta

La Larga, and she felt like a monster – 'Nobody loves me' – she was big on the outside but she felt very small inside. Luckily, Juan Quintana was always there to comfort her: he stroked her endlessly long hair, and when she went to bed, Juan Quintana said goodnight, and tucked her in so she wouldn't get cold. He told her he loved her and kissed her tenderly on the forehead, and Berta would say: 'You're the best father in the world.' But later, when she fell asleep, Berta always had the same dream: she was walking along the street, when suddenly a violent gust of wind pushed her over, she grabbed on to a tree, but the wind laughed at her, and uprooted the tree, and blew her away.

As a child, Berta Quintana had only one friend. Her name was Gracia and her father was Joseph the Carpenter, who was the son of Joseph the Carpenter, and grandson of Joseph the Carpenter (who incidentally made great-grandfather's wooden leg), and so on, and Joseph the Carpenter's eldest son would one day also be called Joseph the Carpenter. There had been so many generations of Joseph-the-Carpenters that they claimed they were related to the first Joseph the Carpenter, the father of Our Lord Jesus Christ. Joseph the Carpenter considered himself an artist, and if he'd been around to see the clay figure of his ancestor made by the first settlers, he'd have had a heart attack.

All the Joseph-the-Carpenters had quite a bit of luck in life. They attributed it to the fact that they spent their days touching wood, which brings very good luck, but Joseph the Carpenter couldn't understand why his daughter, called Gracia because she was born smiling and not crying like other babies, had been a feeble, sickly child since birth. She couldn't run, or play, and very often the poor thing didn't even have the strength to talk. She was always tired and spent long periods in bed, but she never lost her smile. Berta La Larga was the only person of the same age who went to visit her. Gracia could see how sad her friend was and tried to cheer her up (you'd have thought it would be the other way round): 'You're very lucky to be healthy', and Berta really liked being with her. Joseph the Carpenter couldn't understand why his daughter should have to suffer so much, bless her, when he spent his life touching wood and going to church to pray for her. 'She's just a child, she's a saint.' He also prayed to Saint Joseph the Carpenter, as he considered him one of the family: 'You were a father too, at least let her live till the age of thirty-three like your son Jesus Christ.'

But God and Saint Joseph must have been hard of hearing because poor Gracia died when she was only thirteen. She died in her sleep, no trouble to anyone as usual, and she didn't lose her smile even in death, bless her. Joseph the Carpenter wanted to make her the most beautiful coffin in the world. He used a fine piece of oak, and he said: 'Look at the lovely coffin I've made my daughter.'

Berta was as upset by Gracia's death as Joseph the Carpenter. She felt terribly sad, she'd lost her only friend, and she cried, just like the sky, which had since become overcast. Somebody said even the sky was sad and that was why it was raining. Only Juan Quintana was able to comfort his daughter. He told her death was beautiful, because after death we go to heaven: 'One day you'll see Gracia again and all those we've lost.' Berta smiled and thought how she'd see her great-grandfather – she'd heard so much about him. Juan Quintana said that when he died he wanted to be buried with the wooden leg so he could give it back to great-grandfather. 'But he won't need it in heaven,' said Berta, and her father explained that you never know, he just might. From that day on, whenever Berta felt very unhappy, she thought of Gracia, and she wished she could be with her, wherever she was, because she was sure it didn't matter there if you were tall or short.

One day Berta La Larga's father took her to see the travelling circus, where they had human beings on show, and her life would never be the same again. Berta was shocked by the parade of freaks: the bearded lady; the strongest man in the world, who could lift nearly four hundred and fifty pounds; the rubber lady, who could wrap her arms and legs around her body, and also some Siamese twins who shared a torso but had separate arms and legs, and heads, of course. They each had their own husband, and one of them described their incredible lives, and everyone was shocked when they heard that all four of them slept together. But what made the deepest impression on Berta La Larga was seeing a dwarf called Gustavo, billed as the smallest man in the world.

Despite being less than three feet tall, he was the most normal of the lot, and when Berta went over to him, he stared up at her, like someone looking up at a skyscraper, and Berta looked down, as if she were staring into a well. The dwarf must have realized that Berta was sad: 'What's the matter?' 'I don't like being so tall.' 'I don't like being so short, but we can still be happy.' And the dwarf disappeared saying: 'Wait here a moment.' He came back with a woman of the same size. She was so small she looked like a doll, and he said she was his wife. Berta La Larga never forgot Gustavo the dwarf's blue eyes, and she thought that maybe some day she too could be happy. Some day.

But happiness didn't come. Berta Quintana marked her height on her bedroom wall, and every night she checked to see if she'd grown. If she had, she felt miserable and cried; and it made her even sadder when she saw the rain fall inexorably, like her tears. Her father comforted her and stroked her endlessly long hair: 'I'm sure you won't grow any more.' But Berta went on growing until she was the tallest person in Navidad. Juan Quintana's love for his daughter also grew excessively, and to cheer her up he'd say: 'You don't know how lucky you are to be so tall. Don't you see? You're nearer to heaven than the rest of us.' Berta felt better and smiled: he was right. And Juan Quintana took his daughter to the top of the mountain and said: 'No-one's nearer to heaven than you.' And Berta said: 'You're the best father in the world.'

To make matters worse, when she reached adolescence, she was cruelly afflicted with acne, and young men still wouldn't come near her for fear of appearing short beside her and thus being the butt of jokes, and nobody cared what Berta was like inside. Life's so unfair. On top of her problems with men, Berta La Larga had problems with clothes, even the biggest sizes in shops were too small. Her mother had to make clothes for her, and was always lowering the hems of her dresses. She had to buy men's shoes for her, when she could find them, and Juan Quintana had to order a special bed from Joseph the Carpenter so that her feet didn't hang over the end.

Because of her height Berta became a shy, retiring child, who looked down when she was spoken to, and hunched as she walked so she wouldn't stick out so much, always staring down. This meant she became exceedingly well acquainted with the paving stones of the main street. She always won the blindfold-races held during the village *fiestas* because she knew the surface of the street better than anyone, and also because she took the longest strides. Only on these rare days was she glad of being so tall, and on the days when her mother sent her to the grocer's. Dolores was the owner of the grocer's shop, and she sometimes asked Berta to help her get tins off the highest shelves, because Dolores was only four feet five and her shop was so narrow that she had to pile things up to the ceiling – she could only reach the first two shelves. In return for her help, Berta was given sweets. She always asked for mints, they were her favourites. And more often than not she went and ate them in the Corner of Heaven, a place she'd discovered in the forest. She'd called it that because it was a clearing in the middle of the dense forest, like an oasis open to the heavens. It was Berta La Larga's secret place. She spent hours and hours there staring up at the sky, discovering imaginary shapes in the clouds: 'That one looks like a face. That one's like a fish. And that one's like a little bunny rabbit.' And she shared her solitude with the clouds. She also dreamed some day of sharing it with her ideal man. Some day.

But for the time being she had to make do with Alberto the Baker's son, Amadeo the Idiot, who was now nineteen. Only Amadeo seemed not to care that Berta was so tall, but no woman, however desperate, could want a man like Amadeo. The silly fool had declared his love to all the girls in Navidad, not just once but lots of times because he was very forgetful and he never remembered who he had declared his love to. He said: 'I lo-lo-lo-lo-love you.' And he got all nervous and you couldn't understand a word he said. People didn't laugh at him too much because they were afraid of his strength, so they just kept out of his way. Berta La Larga was the kindest to him, perhaps because he was as special as she was, and their loneliness created a bond between them. She was very patient with him, she was teaching him to read and write. He hadn't learnt at school, but thanks to Berta La Larga now at last he could write his name and numbers from one to ten, though he sometimes forgot everything from one day to the next and they had to start all over again. Amadeo the Idiot's parents were very grateful to Berta. In return for the lessons they gave her cakes, as they owned the village cake shop. Afterwards Berta gave the little cakes to Amadeo the Idiot, who was always hungry, and he ate them with such relish it was a pleasure to watch.

He gazed at her, lovestruck, over his letters, and one day he asked her to teach him how to write I love you, and she showed him. So Amadeo the Idiot, who wasn't made of stone, said: 'I lo-lo-lo-lo-lo-love you.' Berta was moved by his words, but she didn't love him back. She took his hand and told him that she loved him like a brother, and he felt happy, because she was the first woman who hadn't laughed at him. He didn't have any brothers or sisters, but now he had a sister. He tried to kiss Berta but she said it couldn't be. 'Wh-wh-wh-why not?' 'Because we're like brother and sister, and brothers and sisters don't kiss.' Amadeo the Idiot took a while to understand this, but at last he saw that Berta was right: if she was like a sister to him she couldn't be his girlfriend. Pity.

Meanwhile, Berta La Larga visited the lovers' tree, and saw the names of all the girls there but her own. One day Amadeo the Idiot followed her to the tree and said he wanted to carve his name next to hers: 'P-p-p-please let me.' Once again she had to remind him that he was like a brother to her, and every time she said it, poor Amadeo the Idiot crumpled. Once again, he declared his love to all the other girls, hoping that they wouldn't turn out to be related to him too, and now he could write a bit, he had fun carving his name next to the names of all the girls in the village.

Only once did a young man other than Amadeo the Idiot seem interested in her. He asked her to go for a walk with him and told her he loved her, and Berta felt happy until she heard the young man's friends laughing and realized it was all a joke. Berta La Larga wanted to die. She ran off into the forest and cried until nightfall. Meanwhile, her parents feared the worst: 'What if she's dead?' And the whole village went to look for her. Luckily, Amadeo the Idiot searched like mad – even though it had started raining, which severely hampered the operation – and at last he found her: she was curled up under a tree, trembling. He carried her back to the village, and Juan Quintana was so grateful that he decided to let Amadeo the Idiot have all the beer he wanted, on the house, for a month.

Juan Quintana cursed all the young men in Navidad, though deep down he was grateful that nature had made sure that no man would want his daughter. He knew it was a selfish thought, but he couldn't help it. Although he couldn't bear having the child suffer because of her height, the thought of Berta with another man was even worse. He loved her more than life itself, maybe because she was his only child and he'd given her all the love he'd have had to share between more children. The mere thought of his daughter with a man made him jealous. He'd say to Roberta: 'I don't care if the child doesn't find a husband. She's better off with us than with a man. He'd probably make her miserable anyway.' Roberta Anaya got angry: 'You're so selfish, Juan Quintana. You should be thinking of your daughter's happiness.' 'Happiness is a load of rubbish. It doesn't exist. We were put on this earth to suffer.' 'Do you want your daughter to end up an old maid?' 'Better an old maid than an unhappy wife.' Berta seemed so fragile, so timid, he felt he had to protect her more and more. He wouldn't let anyone hurt her ever again. 'Just let them try. They'll have to walk over my dead body first.' From then on only Amadeo the Idiot was allowed to go near her: Amadeo was no threat, and he was the one who found her in the forest.

But Juan Quintana knew in his heart of hearts that even though his daughter was so tall, some day she'd meet a man and fall in love. All those years bringing her up and what for? Every night he asked his wife if she knew whether their daughter was going out with any man, and Roberta Anaya said 'no'. As Juan Quintana was sure that the day his daughter did go out with a man his wife wouldn't tell him, he went secretly once a week to the lovers' tree and searched the trunk for his daughter's name, and when he saw it wasn't there, he breathed a sigh of relief. 'Thank God.' Lately, he'd seen Amadeo the Idiot's name next to the name of several girls, and he thought to himself: 'Good for Amadeo, maybe he's not as stupid as he looks.' He knew about all the romantic liaisons in the village, and he told Roberta about them, and she couldn't understand how he was always so well informed. Juan Quintana didn't want his wife to know that he went to the lovers' tree so he said: 'News travels fast in a village.'

Since leaving school at thirteen, Berta La Larga had helped out in the tavern in the mornings – she swept, and dusted the bottles and furniture – and in the afternoons she went to the sewing and cookery classes held in the church which were attended by all young girls of marriageable age. 'You've got to get them ready for married life.' Juan Quintana had been against his daughter preparing for anything, least of all marriage, but Roberta Anaya, who wanted the best for her daughter, said to Juan Quintana, raising her voice for the first time in her life: 'If the child doesn't go to those classes, you can forget about my left breast.' It was one of the few times she spoke angrily to him. Juan Quintana summoned all his pride and said that nobody threatened him, least of all a woman – but he'd never seen Roberta Anaya so determined. He didn't take orders from anyone, least of all his own wife, so he talked himself round: 'We can't keep the child indoors all day, and better that she's with other girls. And that left breast does taste good. Lucky the child didn't get her mother's breasts, or she'd have a lot more suitors by now.'

Roberta Anaya helped at the tavern too, she was in charge of the kitchen. Juan Quintana hardly ever let her out, since it wasn't just his daughter he guarded jealously, and at the tavern most of the customers were men. The Quintana family still lived over the tavern, in the house great-grandfather built, and as they only had one daughter, Juan Quintana let out the spare room, so the tavern was also a hotel, despite Roberta's opposition. As she pointed out, the room wasn't taken very often. She said this not only because there were hardly any guests but because she dreamed of having a room to herself, where she could sew, sit with her friends or just have a break from Juan Quintana: he was very tiresome sometimes, what with his ideas about how to attract customers to the tavern during the week, and his fixation with her left breast on Sundays and holidays. Fortunately, Roberta Anaya had Friday evenings to herself, because the men got together at the tavern to discuss men's things, and they didn't allow women. The women also got together, to talk about women's things and criticize men. They didn't let on to Margarita Cifuentes, but even at home on her own she'd chatter away to the four walls.

And since the age of thirteen, Berta had stayed at home on her own on those nights. She'd lean out of the window and gaze at the stars. 'What's the use of being nearer to heaven if no-one loves me?' She felt terribly unhappy. She was losing hope of ever finding a man to love her.

At the tavern they earned enough to live on but only just, because another tavern had recently opened in the village. And because many of his customers were friends, Juan Quintana had to put their drinks on the slate, which amounted to giving them away free, and they never left tips. It was Berta and her mother who had to pay the consequences: they had to put up with Juan Quintana complaining bitterly about it, with good reason if the truth be told, because not a day went past when he wasn't obliged to give someone a drink on the house.

For instance, Pedro the Blind Man lived off the charity of others. Every evening Juan Quintana had to give him a free brandy, which in fact meant two, because he always dropped his glass on the floor − not just because he was blind, but because he was also terribly clumsy, except when it came to touching women's bottoms, and then he was incredibly dexterous, so much so that people started to doubt he was blind. Their doubts were allayed when one day he touched a man's bottom, and the man got furious, and if Pedro the Blind Man hadn't really been blind, as had just been proved, the man would probably have killed him. He always had his flies open, and he had to be told to do them up, but because he was blind they forgave him everything. The women were so used to seeing his underpants that they weren't shocked, and they even knew exactly what colours they were: lately he'd been wearing green, black and cream, and nobody understood where he got such fancy underwear.

Juan Quintana also felt obliged to provide free drinks to the village mayor, who elected himself − he wasn't the richest man in Navidad for nothing, or rather, the least poor. He had more land than anyone else, but he didn't like working much. What he really liked was drinking. His name was Feliciano, and he drank so as to forget that his wife, Margarita Cifuentes, never stopped talking. She just wouldn't shut up, so everybody avoided her. It was unbelievable how much she talked. They said even dogs ran away from her, and they called her husband Feliciano the Saint because of what he had to put up with. What others said in two words, GOOD MORNING, took for ever with Margarita: 'GOOD heavens, here we are. At least it's fine today, but who knows what'll happen. Men are just like the weather, you can't trust them. That's why I don't let Feliciano look at other women, especially young ones. And have you seen so-and-so's daughter? And I'm going to make such-and-such a stew today . . . Well, good MORNING.'

In a way, even God, in the shape of his envoy, Father Federico, had to put up with Margarita Cifuentes. Hearing her confession was absolute torture. She wasn't a bad person though, she didn't have a lot of sins. Probably her worst sin was being such a pain in the arse. On one occasion, Father Federico fell asleep during her confession, and on another, he just couldn't get her to stop. He'd repeatedly given her his blessing, but she said she hadn't finished yet. The priest wanted to urinate, and he had time to go to the toilet and get back without her noticing. Margarita Cifuentes interspersed her confession with descriptions of recipes, conversations with her husband, the latest fashions in the capital and her family history. Father Federico cast up his eyes: 'So this is earning a place in heaven.'

The only time his wife's verbal diarrhoea worked to the mayor's advantage was when he had to go round collecting taxes, a difficult task since everybody was poor. He got Margarita Cifuentes to accompany him and in 90 per cent of cases they handed over the money: it was better to go hungry than to have to listen to her gabbling. The poor mayor, Feliciano the Saint, was so exhausted when he got to the tavern that Juan Quintana would probably have given him free drinks even if he hadn't been mayor – he deserved it.

And Joseph the Carpenter deserved it too. He never got over the death of his daughter Gracia, having another three children didn't make up for it. He stopped talking to Saint Joseph, and he stopped thinking of him as one of the family: 'She was just a child.' Now, instead of going to church, he went to The Pirate tavern and had a glass of wine. 'Wine does you more good than prayer.' 'Don't blaspheme.' 'It was a blasphemy that God took my daughter.' And every Sunday he went to the cemetery and spoke to the child, bless her. And only Juan Quintana could understand his immense pain; he loved Berta so much he couldn't bear it if she died. And the only thing he could do for Joseph the Carpenter was give him another glass of wine, on the house.

And now he had to give Amadeo the Idiot free drinks too. Since saving Berta he'd developed quite a taste for alcohol. When his month of free drinks for saving Berta was over, he still came to the tavern and asked for a beer, and took the bottle to his lips as clumsily as when he was a baby trying to find the breast, and some of the beer spilled on the floor. He usually did everything slowly but he gulped that beer down in a flash and, emboldened by the alcohol, he grabbed Juan Quintana and lifted him up, and asked for another free beer, and it'd be a brave man who'd dare refuse, because what Amadeo the Idiot lacked in brains he made up for in brawn.

Berta hated working at the tavern, but as a woman and in a village like Navidad, she had no choice but to help with the family business. To make matters worse she had to do what she most hated in the world: the sweeping. And her father forbade her to talk to any of the young men who came, except for the one who least interested her: Amadeo the Idiot.

The only thing that amused her was listening to her father's original ideas for attracting customers – it was a real obsession of his. As tips were so scarce, he rang a cowbell whenever someone deigned to leave something, he wanted everyone to know. And when he wasn't looking, the children had fun ringing the cowbell behind his back. Then they ran away, because Juan Quintana wasn't in the least bit amused. Juan Quintana was very imaginative – he'd have probably gone far if he'd had an education or been born in the city. It had been his idea to have the post delivered to the tavern, so that all the inhabitants of Navidad had to go and fetch their letters from the tavern and maybe have a drink while they were at it. For the last twenty years, every Monday, Wednesday and Friday, the postman had brought the mail to the tavern. They called him the silent postman, because in twenty years, they'd only ever heard him say six words (Margarita Cifuentes, take note): 'good morning' and 'son of a bitch', the last four every time his clapped-out bicycle had a puncture. Once the postman had been, Juan Quintana rang the cowbell to announce the arrival of the post and the villagers came to the tavern, but they rarely stayed for a drink, as Juan Quintana had hoped. It's one thing coming up with ideas, but quite another putting them into practice.

But it was thanks to the tavern and her father's idea of having the post delivered there, that at the age of sixteen Berta Quintana fell in love. And if, as they say, the more impossible the love, the more beautiful, Berta Quintana's romance had everything going for it.

Portrait of Margarita Cifuentes

y all returned home to mourn their dead.

The road that ran between Navidad and Ponsa was in such bad state and had so many bends that the three miles separating the two villages seemed more like six. And if it rained the road became so muddy that three miles seemed to go on for ever. And although Ponsa didn't have any famous sons, or crafts, or local produce, and hadn't witnessed any wars either, it was on the way to somewhere, as it was near the new road that led to the capital, and because of that Ponsa had grown and overtaken Navidad. They didn't have a legend like the one about the Rainbow but since Berta La Larga's birth, this didn't amount to much anyway. Ponsa now appeared on maps in larger lettering than Navidad, and the inhabitants of Navidad were green with envy. They wrote to the National Cartography Department outlining their complaints but they never got an answer.

The inhabitants of Navidad only ever went to Ponsa when absolutely necessary, and it was frowned upon if the young people of the two villages had anything to do with each other. They shared the doctor, and the post arrived in Navidad via Ponsa, which in turn received it from the capital, but other than that they kept their dealings to the minimum.

Berta saw him the first time he came to the village. His name was Jonas and he had just been appointed as the new postman of Ponsa following the enforced retirement of his predecessor, the silent postman, who'd gone to a better place. He wasn't a bad man, but no-one in Navidad mourned his passing because he was from Ponsa, and even if he hadn't been from Ponsa, with only six words in his repertoire he wasn't really going to earn anyone's respect. As the saying went: 'The only good Ponsan is a dead one.'

The new postman arrived on his brand-new bicycle. He took

The rivalry between Navidad and Ponsa was as old as t
two villages themselves, and they had had serious confli
on more than one occasion. It all started over a piece of lar
that didn't belong to anyone. The inhabitants of Navid;
decided it belonged to them, but when the inhabitants of Pon
found out, they wanted it too, and they nearly came to blow
They didn't in the end because the authorities in the capi
intervened, and, following Solomon's example, divided
land into two equal parts. Then a girl from Navidad got pr
nant by a boy from Ponsa, but he didn't want to marry her.
girl took her own life, and the inhabitants of Navidad
over to Ponsa with the intention of killing the bastard
the situation didn't escalate, because the man died of a
attack when he heard the news of the suicide. Th
villages fell silent, not knowing what to say to each oth

almost half an hour to get there because the road really was appalling. When he entered the tavern to deliver the post, Berta La Larga was sweeping. She stopped and stared at him, stunned. For the first time in her life here was somebody taller than her: Jonas was six feet five. He must have been thinking the same because he stared back. For several seconds, their eyes met, more than enough time for Berta to admire his blue eyes. It was like looking at the sky, and it made her feel so happy to look up at another human being for once. Then Juan Quintana appeared. 'You're the new postman.' 'Yes.' 'What's your name?' 'Jonas.' 'That's a strange name.' And the young man handed over the post. Juan Quintana looked him up and down. 'You're very tall. Do you know if your mother ate a lot of yeast when she was pregnant?' Jonas shrugged: 'I don't really understand your question.' He left the tavern, and he and Berta stared at each other again, and that day Berta felt her heart beat nervously, she couldn't stop thinking about Jonas and his eyes as blue as the sky. Then she remembered the dwarf she met at the circus, who told her she could be happy and tall at the same time, and she remembered his blue eyes, they were almost as beautiful as Jonas's. Almost. And so it was that love took over Berta La Larga's life.

Just like the previous postman, Jonas brought the post every Monday, Wednesday and Friday at midday. From the moment they first met, Berta could think of nothing but Mondays, Wednesdays and Fridays, and she hated Tuesdays, Thursdays, Saturdays and Sundays. On Mondays, Wednesdays and Fridays she started sweeping at eleven thirty, just in case he arrived early, and now she loved doing the sweeping. When they saw each other, Jonas looked down, seized with shyness, and Berta did the same, but she had to keep an eye out for Juan Quintana just in case he was watching them. Berta went on sweeping, glancing at Jonas out of the corner of her eye as he handed her father the post, and the tavern had never been as clean in its entire history.

Around that time the weather in Navidad was magnificent, the sky was as clear and blue as Jonas's eyes. Berta felt as radiant as the sun. She walked proudly, her head held high, and she'd never been so pleasant to her neighbours: she greeted them with an almost contemptuously bright smile, she played with the children and helped the old people cross the road, and she even engaged Margarita Cifuentes in conversation. That wasn't difficult of course, Margarita Cifuentes started chattering away nineteen to the dozen: 'You're looking very cheerful. Haven't we had lovely weather lately? I said to Feliciano I thought you were looking very pretty. I'm going to the hairdresser's. My hair's a disaster, styles just don't last when it's this long. I've got to do the shopping, because tomorrow I've got to help Feliciano write some letters and I won't have a spare minute, blah, blah, blah.' So that was the first and last time Berta listened to her ramble on. She might have been in love but she wasn't stupid.

All she could do was think about him, and everything seemed wonderful: animals, life, trees, sunsets. She even found Doña Lucia's singing beautiful. Doña Lucia was a dotty old lady who sometimes took it into her head to sing during the night. She woke the whole village because she started up at three in the morning. She sang so badly that even the children woke up, and it's well known that they sleep very soundly. Someone would have to go to her house and put a hand over her mouth until she shut up. Lots of people asked why didn't they do the same to Margarita Cifuentes.

It was impossible for Jonas to go unnoticed and the news soon spread that the new postman was even taller than Berta La Larga. They started to make jokes about what a good couple they'd make, and if they got married they'd have children over eight feet tall, and from then on they called him Jonas El Largo. When the jokes reached Juan Quintana's ears, he became furious and kicked the tavern door. Roberta Anaya, fearing that Juan Quintana would suffer the same fate as great-grandfather, called Joseph the Carpenter, and they finally managed to calm him down. Everyone was surprised at Juan Quintana's fury, and from then on no-one mentioned the subject, at least not in his presence. Just in case, Juan Quintana gave his daughter a very serious talking-to, he said she mustn't even think of falling in love with the postman, he was from Ponsa for Christ's sake. Berta lied and said she hadn't even noticed him and they'd never said a word to each other (that part was true), and Juan Quintana said if he ever saw them together he'd kill Jonas. But Berta's love was unstoppable, and no-one, not even her own father, could do anything about it.

One day Juan Quintana took Jonas aside and asked Berta to leave. When they were alone he said very firmly that he mustn't even think of courting his daughter. The postman, who realized that Juan Quintana really meant it, answered that he was just doing his job, and that his family would never allow him to have a relationship with a girl from Navidad. From outside on the porch, Berta La Larga tried to hear the conversation between Jonas and her father, but at that moment Amadeo the Idiot came up to her. He was worried by the rumours: 'D-d-d-do do do you have a b-b-boyfriend?' Berta snapped at him for the first time ever: 'You are a nuisance. No, I don't have a boyfriend.' And Amadeo the Idiot was relieved, but sad because of the way Berta had treated him. When Jonas came out of the tavern, his eyes met Berta's, and Amadeo the Idiot, not too pleased, was tempted to trip him up, but stopped himself: 'I don't want Berta telling me off again.'

Even though Berta La Larga and Jonas El Largo had never spoken, they loved each other, silently, and one day, a month and a half after they met, when Jonas arrived at the tavern and walked past Berta, he dropped a letter. Berta La Larga knew it was for her. She picked it up and put it in her pocket, and as soon as Jonas had left, she ran to her room and lay on her bed and read it. It was a very brief letter, all it said was: 'I like you a lot', but to Berta it seemed wonderful, full of feeling. As she read it, she realized how much in love she was. She read it over and over, stroking the words written in ink, and she sighed with love for the first time in her life: 'Isn't his handwriting pretty? Isn't the notepaper lovely? Isn't it wonderful to be alive?' And she hid the letter under her mattress. She thought about how to answer. She didn't dare speak to him, so she decided to write back, and she made over a hundred rough drafts. When she'd settled on the contents, which went, 'I like you a lot too, I haven't stopped thinking about you since I met you, your eyes are wonderful,' she tried different kinds of handwriting, to see which was prettiest. She wrote the letter out in upper case, lower case, italics, and in grown-up handwriting like her mother's, and in the end she chose the simplest. She took five days to write out the final letter. She waited for him on the porch, put the letter down by great-grandfather's leg and signalled with her eyes that it was for him. Jonas picked it up and a few days later he sent her another very similar letter: 'I can't live without you either, you have the most beautiful eyes I've ever seen.' She wrote back, and so on. And so their love began by correspondence.

And now, instead of waiting for him inside the tavern, Berta waited on the porch, sweeping and dusting great-grandfather's leg, so she could give him her letters and receive his, and the porch and great-grandfather's leg had never been so clean.

In his letters Jonas told Berta that he was eighteen years old, lived with his aunt Enriqueta, and that his big ambition was to go and live in the capital and be a bus driver. He told her about all the problems he'd had because of his height, which were very similar to her own, and Berta felt he understood her. She told him what her father said: 'He says that tall people are closer to heaven.' Berta felt reassured when Jonas wrote that he didn't care if she was from Navidad – he'd never understood the rivalry between the two villages – and that he dreamed of buying a motorbike, and liked roast lamb, eggs for breakfast, coffee-flavoured sweets and playing basketball. She also found out that one of his ancestors was Dutch and very tall, and had gone to the Americas to make his fortune, and although he hadn't made his fortune, his eye colour had been passed on to his descendants. Berta thanked God for giving Jonas a Dutch ancestor, for there was no doubt why Jonas's eyes were as blue as the sky.

Now that Berta La Larga knew Jonas liked coffee-flavoured sweets, whenever she went to Dolores's shop to help her stack tins on the highest shelves, she always asked for mints for herself and coffee-flavoured sweets for him. And every time Jonas came to the tavern, she left a coffee-flavoured sweet by great-grandfather's leg, and he took it, and as they still hadn't spoken to each other, he thanked her with a warm smile. From then on, Jonas always left Berta a present too: he put a stamp inside every letter, and that was how Berta found out that Jonas collected them. He'd inherited a collection from his Dutch ancestor, and he dreamed of travelling all over the world. Thanks to Jonas, Berta found out about faraway places, many of which she hadn't even learned about at school. The names of the countries amused her, some of them were so odd. For instance, France reminded her of a pig called 'Franca' that she looked after on her grandparents' farm when she was a child. United States, that was a strange name, and what did that business about being united mean? Maybe there were lots of Siamese twins there, like the ones she saw at the circus.

Liechtenstein, she didn't even want to think about how long it would take Amadeo the Idiot to learn that word. And Iceland, she'd never go somewhere that sounded so cold. Jonas explained things about the countries, and Berta spent hours and hours staring at the stamps. In her imagination she travelled all round the world: she went from France to Italy in the morning, from China to the United States in the afternoon, and from Canada to Egypt before supper. At night she stopped in India, and she fell asleep thinking of how some day she'd travel with her beloved and have the world at her feet. Some day.

Love also gave her a ferocious appetite, she was hungry all the time. Roberta Anaya had never seen her eat so much. She put on several pounds which really suited her, because she had been too thin, and it showed in her face too, she stopped being so pale, she was a very healthy colour now, and even her acne disappeared. Sometimes she woke up at night thinking about him; she'd get out of bed, go straight to the kitchen and eat the first thing she found. When she had the dream about walking along the street and being blown over by a gust of wind, Jonas El Largo appeared. Instead of his bicycle he was riding a white horse, and he saved her, they fell into a wonderful embrace, and held each other so close that not even a hurricane or God himself could pull them apart.

Now when she went to the Corner of Heaven she'd think about him, and she'd search for her beloved's face amongst the clouds, but as the weather was so good at that time there were never enough clouds to form an entire face, and she had to make do with seeing small parts of his body: 'That cloud looks like his mouth, and that one looks like his little finger, and that one's like his nose.' She took his letters with her and read them over and over, and never got bored with them. Even though she knew the contents by heart, she never tired of stroking the paper that he'd touched, or of staring at the words that he'd written out of love. Some day she would share the Corner of Heaven with him, and she ticked off the minutes till she next saw him in a little notebook, as if she were a captive, which is exactly what she was, a prisoner of love. The seconds seemed like hours, hours like whole days, and when at last Berta saw him again, she was already suffering, thinking of how short their meeting would be. And then the waiting began all over again, isn't suffering wonderful? She felt so happy that she went to the village church to thank God for having met Jonas. It was the second time she'd had a reason to thank God. The first was when she was thirteen and hadn't grown a fraction of an inch for three months, but when she measured herself again the following month she was two inches taller: she'd never grown so much in one month. But now she was in love she firmly believed in God again, and she only asked for one thing: 'Please make my father let me go out with Jonas.' Young Father Federico saw how happy Berta looked and was convinced that the transformation was due to his advice and the great efforts he'd made to cheer her up. He was especially fond of her. When he first met her, she was a vulnerable little girl, with sad eyes, but now she looked happy and confident. Women were a mystery to Father Federico, he never understood them. He'd become a priest not because of a single woman, but because of lots. He was the only boy in a family of seven girls, his mother was a widow, and his two spinster aunts lived with them too. The young Federico lived in a hen coop of ten women, sometimes they all talked at once, and in the end he'd had quite enough of women. When he decided to become a priest, it upset his mother terribly as their surname wouldn't be passed on. She'd always dreamed of having lots of granddaughters – she preferred girls – and a daughter-in-law whom she'd love like a daughter.

Amadeo the Idiot noticed how happy Berta was as well, he saw it in her face, and he said: 'Y-y-y-you look so p-p-p-pretty.' But as he was so dense, it didn't even occur to him that she might be in love, despite the rumours: 'She t-t-t-told me herself: I d-d-d-don't have a boyfriend.' During their lessons, Berta was absent-minded, and all the letters of the alphabet reminded her of Jonas: J for Jonas, L for love, K for kiss, F for falling in love, H for happiness, S for sky, M for marriage, and she made herself dizzy thinking about him, she just couldn't concentrate, and she ended up teaching Amadeo very little. Amadeo the Idiot wasn't complaining, it meant he didn't have to study. And now Berta did eat the cakes that Amadeo's mother, Remedios, gave her, she was always starving and she told him she needed to eat, and Amadeo the Idiot stared at her strangely, because she didn't eat them, she devoured them.

Berta La Larga wanted to make herself look pretty for him. She'd never taken so long to get ready, and she asked her mother to make her more dresses, and she put on some of Roberta Anaya's lipstick, but when she saw herself in the mirror she thought it made her look peculiar and she decided to take it off for fear of appearing ridiculous, but especially for fear that her father might see. She tried out lots of different hairdos but she didn't find one that suited her. She also padded out her bra to make her breasts appear larger, like her mother's, but she made such a poor job of it that when she put on her dress to see how she looked, the padding slipped, and when she saw her reflection in the mirror she got quite a fright, it looked as if she had three breasts: her own two and the lump of cotton wool in the middle. And what with one thing and another, she'd spend hours and hours locked in the bathroom. Juan Quintana would bang on the door to get in, and so as not to arouse his suspicions, she said she had a very bad stomach ache, and with her mouth made such loud farting sounds that her father became quite alarmed.

Roberta Anaya was the first to realize that Berta had fallen in love. It was pretty obvious: the child had her head in the clouds all day, she was eating so much, she'd never taken so long to get dressed, her eyes shone and she had a permanent smile on her face. She sang in the bath, and you had to say everything twice: 'Berta, are you listening to me?' She asked Berta if she was in love. At first the child wouldn't tell her anything, in case she told her father, but then she hugged her mother, she needed to confide in her, and she told her she'd fallen in love with Jonas: 'I'm so happy, I love him, please don't tell father.' When she saw how much in love Berta was, her mother swore not to say anything to Juan Quintana: 'I'm sure your father will never let you get engaged and it's even less likely if the boy is from Ponsa.' But from then on the mother became the daughter's confidante: 'Be careful with men, all they want is sex.' Berta wanted to know how her parents had fallen in love, and Roberta Anaya, smiling nostalgically, said Juan Quintana fell in love with her eyes.

Fortunately Juan Quintana didn't find out about Berta falling in love, though he had his suspicions, the child was behaving so strangely. He mentioned it to Roberta Anaya, and she managed to convince him that Berta wasn't in love: 'She's just going through a difficult stage.' That day, just in case, Juan Quintana went to check the lovers' tree. When he didn't find Berta's name there, he breathed a sigh of relief. There was Amadeo the Idiot's name taking up half the trunk, at this rate he'd need a whole tree to himself.

Querido Jonas:

Querido Jonas:

QUERIDO JONAS:

Querido Jonás:

Querido Jonas:

QUERIDO JONAS:

quexido Jonás:

Querido Jonas:

Querido Jonas:

QUERIDO JONAS:

Querido Jonas:

Querido Jonás:

*The different handwriting styles tried out by Berta La Larga
for writing to her beloved*

It was now three months since Berta and Jonas had first met. They still hadn't spoken to each other, nor had they had the slightest physical contact, not even when exchanging letters, as they left them by great-grandfather's leg for fear that Juan Quintana might see them. And in those three months, Jonas had earned the villagers' respect, even though he was from Ponsa, because, although he was just as quiet as the other postman, he was a fine-looking young man and never bothered anyone. Even Juan Quintana was friendly to him, now he was sure there was nothing between Jonas and his daughter.

Until, one day, the two young people came face to face just when Juan Quintana decided to nip to the bathroom after collecting the post, seeing as the child wasn't in there for once. It was then that Berta La Larga decided to hand Jonas her letter personally, and they touched for the first time. Berta's fingers brushed his, and she felt fire, electricity, sparks, fireworks, but just at that moment, with impeccable timing, Amadeo the Idiot appeared: 'H-H-Hello B-B-B-Berta.' Jonas started and ran away. Berta wanted to scold Amadeo, but she couldn't get out a single word: she'd lost the power of speech. She stared in amazement at the hand touched by her beloved, and she started to feel unbearably hot all over. She felt her forehead, which was boiling, and so were her arms, her torso, her legs. She didn't even hear Amadeo the Idiot ask: 'Wh-wh-wh-what's the m-m-m-m-matter?' She went to her room and it was as if an army of drops of sweat were marching all over her body, and she wanted to make love to him, and caress him. Her desire was so strong she felt ashamed, because she'd been taught that sex only came after marriage, and she didn't even dare tell her mother what had happened to her. She locked herself in the bathroom and stood under the shower, and cooled down, but only temporarily, because a few minutes after getting out of the shower she was bathed in sweat again.

From that time on, the temperature in Navidad rose at an incredible rate and went on rising during the following days until it became unbearable. There were no longer any children playing in the street, or dogs wandering about, or old people going for walks, or women having their mid-morning natter. The little breeze there was brought no relief because it was so hot it was unpleasant. Already slow by nature, the villagers now did everything at a pace more befitting to a snail than a member of the human race – several times there was almost an accident in the street – and they could barely do any work. The only thing that brought relief was a good soak in very cold water, and some people took three baths a day, which was unheard of in Navidad, as it was a well-known fact that the villagers disliked bathing. But now most of them took baths daily, when previously they only had one or two baths a week.

Being blind, Pedro the Blind Man had a highly developed sense of smell, and he was going crazy because, despite the fact that the inhabitants of Navidad were bathing as never before, the smell was atrocious, and he fainted several times. He held his nose wherever he went, and had his flies undone as usual, but now he took no notice when they told him to do them up, and unbuttoned his shirt as well: 'Let's see if it cools me down, I could certainly do with it.'

Berta and the women of Navidad spent all day fanning themselves. So did the men. At first they did it in secret, because fanning yourself was a woman's thing, but soon they were prissily fanning themselves in public, anything for some relief from the heat. Some husbands made their wives fan them, and some parents made their children fan them, and Amadeo the Idiot fanned himself with such vigour that he broke several fans belonging to his mother. Remedios was in despair over her son because he couldn't do anything right, and she'd say: 'For my son there is no remedy.'

Many crops were lost, particularly fruit, being the most delicate. It shrivelled from lack of water and fell off the trees, and pretty rotten it must have been too, because the ants and other insects that would normally have had quite a banquet, wouldn't touch it. Other foods also went bad, from one day to the next, even though they were kept in refrigerators. Dolores the Grocer received a huge number of complaints: 'The tuna you sold us is off.' 'The tuna was perfect, it's this damned heat.' Poor Dolores was in despair because she could see her business going to ruin, and one day when Berta went in to do some shopping she caught her fanning the lettuces. She'd also been seen fanning tomatoes, and preserves, which certainly weren't living up to their name. As a result of the rotten foods there were several cases of food poisoning – the worst affected was Amadeo the Idiot because he'd stuffed himself, and he spent several days throwing up, so luckily nobody else felt much like eating. Berta La Larga lost all the weight she'd put on, and started giving her cakes to Amadeo the Idiot again because however much in love she was, she simply couldn't eat in such suffocating heat. He was more grateful than ever for the cakes, because after all the vomiting he was absolutely starving.

At night the temperature increased even more, like Berta's desire. She longed to touch him, to feel his skin, to kiss him deeply, she even wanted to lick him and she hugged her pillow; she pretended it was him, and kissed the pillow and, at dawn, when she fell asleep at last, he'd appear in her dream about the tree and save her, but this time they made love, their bodies intertwined, and Juan Quintana saw them and tried to kill Jonas. And she woke up with a start, screaming, with the sheets completely soaked.

Like Berta La Larga, many of the inhabitants of Navidad, who normally slept like logs, started to suffer from insomnia as never before. You could hear the children crying and the dogs howling, but at least Doña Lucia felt too stifled to sing. The men took hours and hours to make love to their wives, because it was so hot they moved very slowly, more conscious of their own sweatiness than of any pleasure, and on top of that they were losing all the water they'd drunk during the day, and the sheets were soaked. Pools of sweat formed beside the beds, it was like being in a sauna and, of course, they lost the urge to make love a second time. During those days, the men and women, particularly the married ones, lost weight at an extra-ordinary rate. And since they made love with the windows wide open, their panting could be heard all over the village. Berta put her head under the pillow so she couldn't hear, because she felt the same desire as her elders. 'I want to make love to you, Jonas.'

Juan Quintana spent his nights pacing up and down the

bedroom, and practically wore out the wooden floor. He tried everything to get himself off to sleep: walking several miles before bedtime to tire himself out, replacing coffee with herbal tea, counting sheep, dogs, cockerels, breasts. In the end he decided to count customers, it was more fun. He counted so many he could have filled over a hundred taverns like his. He advised his daughter to count something or other to get herself off to sleep, and she took his advice – she counted the seconds till she saw her beloved again. Juan Quintana was in such a state because of the heat that he didn't even feel like sucking Roberta's left breast. In the many hours in which he was now free to think, he had an idea for making the heat stop, and the whole village applauded it: they would let Doña Lucia sing, as there was a famous saying that people who sang badly brought on rain. So, at first with delight and then out of duty, poor Doña Lucia sang for almost an entire week until she completely lost her voice. And still it didn't rain, and on top of that the villagers were exhausted from putting up with her singing. Berta was the only one who didn't mind listening to her warbling because, in spite of everything, even the unbearable heat, the world seemed wonderful: trees, flowers, wind, even sweat. But to get a break from the heat, during the day she went to Canada – according to her beloved, it was always very cold there – and imagined she was sitting on snow, which in fact melted within a few minutes. She gave up her exotic nights in India and spent the night in Russia instead. But she still couldn't sleep.

Of all of them, it was the mayor, Feliciano the Saint, whose insomnia was worst, because his wife, Margarita Cifuentes, couldn't sleep either and she wouldn't stop talking: what a nightmare. On top of that, at about three in the morning she'd get all transcendental on him: 'Where do we come from? Where are we going? What are we struggling for? Feliciano, are you listening to me?' Although he then fell asleep exhausted, he woke up in the morning with a terrible headache. During the day they were overcome with tiredness and it made them all rather touchy. There had never been so many rows, between married couples, parents and children, shopkeepers and customers. Alberto the Baker was the most irritable and it was his son Amadeo who had to pay for his ill humour, he'd never been smacked round the head so often. Thank goodness for the *siesta*, the only time they got any rest; made drowsy by lunch and stupefied by the unbearable, midday heat, they all fell asleep. And even the animals were irritable; dogs bit their owners, the milk from the cows came out sour, and in their obligatory woolly coats, more than one, unable to stand the heat, died of dehydration, and they had to shear them before they were all wiped out. The women had never had to do so much washing, and it dried at an almost supernatural rate: knickers and bras in only five minutes, sheets and towels in twenty minutes, trousers in fifteen.

Juan Quintana was one of the few people to benefit from the heat, as his neighbours came to the tavern to quench their thirst as never before. It was partly thanks to the doctor who treated the inhabitants of Navidad. He was called out on several occasions to treat cases of dehydration and he told them very seriously they had to drink at least three litres of liquid a day, something they weren't accustomed to doing: 'We'll start spawning frogs if we drink that much.' 'That's better than dying of dehydration.' They were fed up with water, so even the women, who normally didn't set foot in the tavern, now went in to buy drinks, and many of them tasted alcohol for the first time in their lives: 'Let's see if it takes our minds off this damned heat.' As they weren't used to it, some of them got drunk: it was funny to see them so animated, but while they forgot the heat for a few hours, what a hangover the following day. Even Juan Quintana declared he would have preferred fewer customers and a slightly more bearable temperature, which showed how hot it was.

And on Mondays, Wednesdays and Fridays, just before she started sweeping, Berta had a shower, and rubbed herself down so hard it hurt. She wanted to smell nice, and now, together with the coffee-flavoured sweet, she had a glass of water ready for Jonas and left it by great-grandfather's leg. Her beloved arrived soaked in sweat after his long journey, he couldn't have smelled worse; but Berta La Larga was so much in love she didn't notice, and Jonas thanked her for the water not only with a look, since they still hadn't spoken, but also with a smile of pleasure as he drank the water. And even though she wanted to touch him, Berta didn't dare, because of her father but also because she feared her body would catch fire. When she saw him, her heart beat so hard she was afraid it might burst. The beating of her heart was quite audible, and so as not to arouse suspicion, when Berta sensed there might be a silence, she hummed the first tune that came into her head.

During Amadeo's writing lessons, the letters continued to remind Berta of her sensual desires: C for caress, N for naked, T for touch, M for making love, L for lust, S for skin, sex and snoring – this last one, although not exactly lewd like the others, came to her because, in the heat, Amadeo fell asleep so soundly that he actually snored. Usually he thoroughly enjoyed ringing the church bells, but he didn't feel like ringing them now: 'I'm so t-t-t-tired.' Father Federico had to push him into the bell tower, and Amadeo had to have a rest between chimes – when he had to ring twelve o'clock it was torture.

It wasn't only Juan Quintana's tavern that was packed out: the other place to benefit from the high temperatures was the village church, watched over by the Pink Virgin of Navidad, thus named because of her pink garb. The villagers took refuge inside the cool church, and many of them, not keen church-goers, now entered the place for the first time in many years. While they were there they asked Father Federico if he could have a word with the Virgin and get her to ask God if he could stop it being so hot (and somebody also said could she, while she was at it, ask God to make Margarita Cifuentes shut up). Father Federico had never had so many people in his church. They were mostly men looking for a shady corner, chatting about their own things, work, women, everything, as if they were at Juan Quintana's tavern. Father Federico would ask them to have a little respect: 'You're in The Lord's house,' and they'd answer sarcastically: 'Well, tell The Lord to give us a bit of cool air.' And even though he knew they weren't there out of piety, Father Federico was happy to see a large congregation in his church for once; it was his first triumph since his ordination, a little over a year ago.

Navidad was the young priest's first post. The villagers were delighted with him because he didn't bully those who didn't go to church every Sunday, unlike the previous priest, who went to their houses to fetch them to Mass. Claiming they didn't know the time because the village clock wasn't working had been to no avail, and he always gave them a hard time in his sermons: 'You'll end up in hell.' It was all sin and blasphemy, and the Devil was everywhere, even in the stew, and his sermons were so apocalyptic that some villagers stopped paying attention, even when he said they only remembered God when they needed something, which was actually entirely true.

Ever since the weather had turned so terribly hot, all the villagers had been watching Father Federico's namesake, Federico the donkey. It must be said that he was named before the priest's arrival in Navidad – he was given the name because he was born on the 7th of October, Saint Federico's day.

According to a local legend, asses could predict the weather. They'd had to go to the capital to buy him because there weren't any asses in Navidad, at least not of the animal kind. The belief was that when he shook his ears it meant rain; if he brayed it was going to turn cold, and if he rolled around on the ground, the weather would be fine. They all watched Federico the donkey and waited for him to bray or shake his ears, in the hope it meant bad weather was on the way, but nothing: the silly ass spent his days rolling on the ground, and as it hadn't rained for so long, he raised a great cloud of dust. If only it had been a rain-cloud. But the temperature went on rising, and reached such extremes that someone said they'd even seen a few drops of sweat on the Pink Virgin, and one irreverent individual suggested removing her pink mantle to cool her down a bit. 'This heat's going to kill us, how long is it going to go on?'

It went on until another event changed the course of the story: one morning Jonas decided he was going to touch his beloved again. After handing over the post, he heard Juan Quintana say he was going to the toilet. As Jonas came out of the tavern, he looked to see if there was anyone around, and then he took Berta's hand, and once again she felt fire and electricity and sparks and fireworks. But the pyrotechnics only lasted a split second, because Roberta Anaya was in the toilet Juan Quintana came out onto the porch and saw them together. Jonas moved away from Berta and rushed off. The father glared at his daughter, thinking the worst. Berta La Larga had to swear fifteen times that there was nothing going on between them. In fact, Juan Quintana hadn't seen them touch, or speak to each other but, just in case, he decided not to let Berta work in the tavern any more, at least not for a time. She was always in a daze lately, and what with the heat as well she didn't get much sweeping done anyway.

When he told her, Berta wanted to cry at the thought that

she wouldn't get to see her beloved, but she restrained herself so as not to arouse Juan Quintana's suspicions. Without a word, she went upstairs to her room and locked herself in. For the first time in her life, she hated her father – because of him she wouldn't see her beloved, and she was so furious that for a few moments she forgot about Jonas.

At the exact moment that Berta became angry, turbulent clouds filled the sky, battling for a space in the firmament. While this was happening, Juan Quintana was checking to see if his daughter's name had been carved on the lovers' tree. And he had a doubly pleasant surprise. First, Berta's name was nowhere to be seen, and second, the clouds brought a lovely cool breeze. And like Juan Quintana, the inhabitants of Navidad, who hadn't seen clouds for so long, stared open-mouthed at the sky, just as they had the day Berta was born and the Rainbow appeared.

That night, Berta La Larga fell asleep thinking about her father and what he'd done to her and how much she hated him. When Juan Quintana came into her room to say goodnight, Berta turned her face away and had to make a huge effort not to cry.

But in the morning Berta couldn't contain herself: she awoke with eyes full of tears, she couldn't bear not to see her beloved. Then Roberta Anaya came in to her room euphoric, and told her to get up and look outside because it was about to start raining. The sky was so black the clouds looked like huge rocks. Berta turned away: who cared about the rain? She didn't want to see anyone except Jonas. Her mother had to drag her out of bed and force her to get dressed. The entire village had turned out to welcome the rain. After such a long drought it was a great event for all of them.

Berta La Larga was the first person to feel a drop of rain, as she was the tallest and closest to the sky, and after her they all felt the water cooling their bodies. The drops tasted glorious, and the children shouted for joy and ran about in the rain, and even the dogs wagged their tails enthusiastically. The church bells rang as Amadeo the Idiot pulled the rope with all his might and shouted like a madman, so that Father Federico had to calm him, just in case the bell crashed down on Amadeo's head. And Juan Quintana was so happy that he let the children ring the tavern cowbell.

Pedro the Blind Man was pleased, mainly for the sake of his nose, but since his sense of touch was also more developed, he felt immense pleasure when the first drop landed on his body, as if the most sensual woman in the world was caressing him. He almost became aroused, until he remembered his flies were undone. It was the only time he was seen doing them up without having to be told.

Federico the donkey stopped rolling about on the ground, not because the fine weather was coming to an end, as would have been logical, but because the ground was wet and he hated water. And then he started shaking his ears, which was a sign of rain, but in fact he was trying to get the water out, and then he rolled about on the ground again, which was an indication either that the donkey wasn't quite right in the head, or that he was no better at predicting the weather than any other inhabitant of Navidad.

Making the most of the fact that, like everyone else, Juan Quintana was in an excellent mood, Berta La Larga picked up the broom and started to sweep the porch. She was sure her father had forgotten the incident with Jonas the day before. But he hadn't. Juan Quintana said he didn't want to see her around the tavern. Berta's protests and Roberta Anaya's intervention were futile. Berta locked herself in her room again. She felt terribly unhappy, and she cried, and she didn't want to see anyone, not even her mother. She cried till the following day, which was Wednesday.

From the window she saw the postman walking up to the tavern in the rain. Seeing him from a distance was even worse, it made her even sadder. She began to cry harder, she'd never been so unhappy in her life. Roberta Anaya tried to comfort her, but without success; and Berta begged her mother not to say anything to her father. Whenever Juan Quintana came into her room, she put her head under the pillow so he wouldn't see her tears, and she told him she had a headache and asked him to leave. Juan Quintana couldn't bear to see his daughter suffer, but he comforted himself with the thought that she seemed to have got over her constipation at least, because she wasn't spending so long in the bathroom now.

Since Berta La Larga started feeling so sad, it rained harder in Navidad, and it continued for several weeks, the sky as black as the first day; even the oldest inhabitants couldn't remember anything like it and they wondered where the blue sky had gone. Blue had become the colour of hope. The sky was black for so long that some of them forgot it had ever been any other colour, but Berta La Larga would never forget, she just had to close her eyes and picture her beloved's blue gaze.

The rain fell relentlessly and flooded everything, first streets, then houses, fields, farms. The inhabitants of Navidad spent all their time filling buckets with water and then emptying them; even during the few hours they were asleep, they dreamed they were still filling and emptying buckets. They woke up hoping it had all been a dream. But it was still raining. Desperate and powerless, the women watched as their houses, their lives, the little they owned were swept away, and they cried so hard people feared they'd make the flood worse.

The children were fed up with being indoors all day, and they wanted to help too, so they blew in the general direction of the sky with all their might to try to push the clouds away. Pedro the Blind Man insisted on helping, but what with his clumsiness and his blindness, he was more a hindrance than a help: he filled up buckets and emptied them in the same place, but it was no use telling him where to empty them. It's the thought that counts.

After prayers Father Federico would go to help the most needy. He rolled up his sleeves just like everyone else, and as his cassock got wet, he hitched up his skirts. Some villagers were shocked at the sight of his legs – he had a very fine pair by the way – but they didn't say anything because his help was much needed, just like everyone else's.

Amadeo the Idiot behaved like a real hero during those days. Being so strong, he did as much work as three beefy men. He helped move furniture, which he loaded on his back all on his own, although some of the furniture did get broken, because he wasn't terribly careful. His mother, Remedios, felt proud of him for the first time, because everybody was congratulating him for all his help, and even his father, Alberto the Baker, who'd always disowned him, now boasted about his son.

As houses became flooded, families took refuge on the upper floors. A symphony of drips could be heard all over the place, day and night, the sound of dripping water never stopped, and many villagers became quite obsessed with it. They covered their ears but they could still hear it, and they started to think they were going mad. The water was already one and a half feet deep, so the animals had to be moved to the upper floors, and Joseph the Carpenter fixed together several strips of wood to build himself a vessel, which he used to get from one end of the village to the other. And, as many villagers wanted to do the same, he had to build some more, and Navidad started to look like Venice, albeit a rather down-market version.

Like his neighbours, Juan Quintana moved his furniture upstairs. He moved the bar and all the bottles and the kitchen units, and the pots and pans and great-grandfather's leg, just in case, and for any neighbours who didn't have an upper floor, he moved all their belongings up there as well. He spent all day bailing out water, and at night he collapsed into bed and fell asleep exhausted. He must have been very tired because he didn't even have the energy to go to Berta La Larga's room and say good night, or even to suck Roberta's left breast. But it didn't escape Juan Quintana's notice that the child simply wouldn't come out of her room, and it reawakened his suspicions that his daughter was in love, but he was too busy with the tavern, and in all that rain he'd never have got as far as the lover's tree anyway.

A few days after it started raining, the village was cut off by the floods; the road that ran between Navidad and Ponsa was more like a river than anything else. And the post no longer came, which meant Jonas didn't either.

Berta Quintana's heart ached, and the distance that separated her from her beloved pained her, and her head ached from thinking about him so much; she was truly lovesick. She alone knew that her pain was infinitely greater than that of the whole village. She hadn't seen her beloved for more than two weeks and she thought she was going to die from love. Her heart beat anxiously: what if it was raining even harder in Ponsa and Jonas had drowned? Meanwhile, Juan Quintana was becoming seriously worried about his daughter. He said if she really wanted to she could come back to work in the tavern, but by then it was too late. Without Jonas, the world had no meaning. And anyway the tavern was flooded.

She just had to see him, and she made three attempts to do so. The first was one night, while her parents were asleep: she took a candle to light her way, but with the water up to her knees, it was almost impossible to walk. On top of that it was dark, and she stumbled and fell, candle and all. She just couldn't see a thing, and when she realized how dark it was she gave up and returned home soaked to the skin. She went straight up to her room, making sure her parents didn't see her, and got into bed without drying herself – it was a miracle she didn't catch her death of cold. Her second attempt was during the day: she got as far as the outskirts of the village, stumbling and falling over as she went, and she got completely drenched again. A neighbour told Juan Quintana he'd seen his daughter trying to leave the village and the father rushed out to find her. He climbed aboard the raft that Joseph the Carpenter had built him, and sailed up the street-cum-river using his hands as paddles, and finally he reached her. Juan Quintana was very cross, and Berta said she couldn't bear being cooped up in the house all day. 'I could do without this kind of nonsense young lady.'

She made a third attempt the following day, but her father caught her again. He was losing patience, and Berta burst into tears in front of him, she didn't care if he saw. She wanted to hug him and tell him she couldn't live without her beloved, but all Juan Quintana could think about was the damned tavern, and Berta cursed the tavern, and she tried to get away from him and run off. Juan Quintana held onto her with all his might: 'What is the matter with you?' Berta started hitting him in fury. Juan Quintana couldn't understand the child. He had to give her a slap to calm her down, and he fell silent as he did so because he'd never hit Berta before. Berta too was stunned. She felt she hated him for the second time in her life, and she told him so: 'I hate you. I hate you.' Juan Quintana had one of the most unpleasant shocks of his life when he heard his daughter's words, because he loved her so much.

He decided to lock her up this time, in the pantry, because the child's bedroom was crammed with chairs and other things from the tavern, and she could escape out of the window. Juan Quintana was horrified that he'd hit her and locked her up, because he loved her so much; and Roberta Anaya defended her daughter, but Juan Quintana wouldn't budge: 'That child gives us nothing but trouble.' He was fed up with hearing that she was at a difficult age.

Locked in a pantry barely more than two metres square, Berta La Larga felt she was the unhappiest woman in the world. She thought of committing suicide, she couldn't live without her beloved, and she hated her father with all her might: he'd hit her, how could he? She looked round to try to take her mind off things but it only made it worse: she felt unhappier than the tomatoes, hazelnuts, *chorizo*, potatoes, onions, almonds, and all the other stuff in that damned pantry.

And while Berta wept tears of love, the sky shed millions of celestial tears. The rain was falling so hard that the villagers feared for their lives, and some thought the Ponsans must have put a curse on them, or that God was angry, and they wondered what crime they'd committed. Others believed it was a manifestation of the proverbial wrath of God, and maybe the previous parish priest was right. Fearing that the whole world was going to be flooded, someone suggested building a great big ship, just like Noah, and saving two animals, one male, one female, of each species. But this was rather silly since they only had pigs, dogs, sheep, cows and hens and Federico the donkey, and he didn't have a mate anyway. He'd been braying for the past few days – yet more proof that he wasn't quite right in the head, because, according to the saying, when donkeys brayed it meant there would soon be fine weather, and the weather in Navidad had never been so bad.

Berta La Larga discovered that eating was the only thing that soothed her aching heart, and through her tears she wolfed down the entire contents of the pantry, which were considerable, since it was the pantry for the tavern. That was how she put on over three kilos in a single week and also how she came to try whisky for the first time. She thought it tasted terrible, but it must have gone to her head because she started to laugh, then sob hysterically, so she ate some cinnamon sweets she found in a jar. She didn't know, of course, that cinnamon is an aphrodisiac, and it awakened her sexual appetite and she wanted to hug him, touch him, make love to him, her desire much stronger than when the weather was too hot. She wanted to eat Jonas up, as if she were a female cannibal: 'I bet his flesh is tastier than the most exquisite delicacy.' She licked her lips at the thought of how tasty his thighs, arms, nose would be. 'My God, I'm going mad.'

Then she saw an ant, which was an unusual sight recently as

it seemed as if the rain had swept away all small creatures. The ant was probably searching for food, and under different circumstances Berta would have killed it, but she couldn't now because she felt as lonely and wretched as the ant: 'Why is life so unfair?'

Juan Quintana deeply regretted what he'd done to his daughter, but the child had given him no choice, and now she wouldn't talk to him. Almost every hour he sent in Roberta Anaya to see how she was. He was so upset he didn't even care that the tavern was sinking under water, the only thing he was concerned about was getting his daughter's love back, which meant that even though he was terribly tired, he couldn't sleep at night. Even Roberta Anaya realized how bad her husband felt and she tried to make Berta see reason: 'You have to forgive your father, then he'll let you out of the pantry.' But the daughter felt hurt and didn't want to forgive him. Berta could think of nothing but Jonas and she asked her mother to bring her beloved's letters. So when she wasn't eating, she read Jonas's letters over and over, and a tear dropped onto one of the letters and the ink ran and turned into a blue tear, as blue as Jonas's eyes. She was going mad locked up in there, and she spent her time counting her tears, counting over one thousand two hundred and ninety five in a single hour, and without realizing she started talking aloud: 'I love you Jonas, I can't live without you, and if I'm never going to see you again, I'd rather die.' Berta saw one of her tears drop onto the ant, and the tiny animal struggled fiercely so as not to drown in the teardrop – she held out her finger to try to save it but she squashed it by mistake. Life is so unfair.

The church in Navidad and the Pink Virgin were the villagers' last remaining hope. Thank God someone had put a plastic cover over her and despite countless leaks throughout the church, the Pink Virgin still presided over her house with dignity. With a faith renewed due to the strange weather they'd been having lately, men and women asked if she could please make it stop raining for Heaven's sake. The rain had no respect even for the house of the Lord, and there was nothing holy about the water pouring in, and they all prayed: 'Thy will be done on earth as it is in Heaven.' And they stressed: 'On earth as it is in HEAVEN.' Of course every cloud has a silver lining: Margarita Cifuentes spent all day in church praying, so at least the mayor, Feliciano the Saint, had a break from her verbal diarrhoea for a few days. But the person who prayed the most during that period was old Inés. She lived in the little house beside the church, where Father Federico lived, and she did the housekeeping for him. She was the most devout person in the village, even though God, in whom she so fervently believed, had taken away her husband and three children in a rather unfortunate fire, and most of the villagers couldn't understand why she still believed.

Berta couldn't take any more: if the rain didn't stop soon it would be the death of her. She asked God with greater fervour than anyone else if He could make it stop raining and in return she'd do anything He wanted. But while she was praying she sucked another of those cinnamon sweets and again she wanted to make love to Jonas, and she felt guilty because she was thinking about God at the same time and she knew He wouldn't like that. Then Berta had the idea of making a promise in return for it stopping raining, and this was her promise: she'd remain a virgin until Jonas and she were married, 'I swear I will, God.' And as she made her promise, she had a ray of hope. After her long period of despair, she now smiled timidly.

The same day, exhausted from all her praying, old Inés also made a promise – but to the Pink Virgin – on behalf of all the villagers. If it stopped raining, they would wear pink for the next year as a sign of their gratitude. And they all applauded her idea, because in the state they were in they would have agreed to anything as long as it stopped raining.

Suddenly, a ray of sun peered out between the clouds. They were all bowled over when they saw it. The clouds began to move away as if by magic, and even Margarita Cifuentes fell silent, an unequivocal sign that what was happening was truly momentous. A few hours later the rain became lighter and then stopped altogether. Who knows whether it was because of the old woman's promise, or Berta's, or nature itself, which, as we all know, is so capricious.

And the sun shone once more in the kingdom of the heavens. The villagers gazed up at it in the same way that they'd have probably looked upon God Himself. They went outside and celebrated till dawn, unaware that their lives were about to change radically. They all hugged, they all loved one another. Some knelt on the still-wet ground and, looking up at the sky, gave thanks. They all congratulated old Inés and chanted her name in unison: her faith had saved them. Meanwhile, Pedro the Blind Man said he too had seen the sun – but nobody believed him, because he was still claiming he could see it when it got dark and, when all the women hugged him, his hands wandered, and they said: 'Don't be disgusting.' And they walked away. 'And do up your flies.'

From her prison, Berta La Larga heard the rain stop and her neighbours shout for joy. She looked up and thanked God for hearing her promise. Then the door to the tiny room opened and there was Juan Quintana. Father and daughter looked into each other's eyes. They fell into a long embrace, full of love, and they asked each other's forgiveness: 'I love you, daughter.' 'I love you too.' And Roberta Anaya watched, deeply moved, because she knew how much they loved each other. And, united once more, the Quintana family went outside to celebrate with the rest of the village.

Moved, Berta looked up at the blue sky, which was the same blue as Jonas's eyes: 'Where are you Jonas?' Although they all said it had stopped raining because of old Inés promise to the Virgin, Berta knew it was because of her own promise, and again she thought about Jonas.

Amadeo the Idiot felt immensely happy, because people had never been so affectionate towards him. They were grateful to him for all his help during the floods, and he was so overcome he couldn't speak. He stammered words that nobody could understand, but they were probably happy words, and what he most enjoyed was being hugged by all the girls who usually shunned him. But that day the hug that made him happiest was from Alberto the Baker, and for the first time in his life he felt the warmth of a father's love. And for the first time in Alberto the Baker's life he felt the warmth of a son's love. And although he normally spent his days working so he could avoid everyone, that day he took a break and joined in the general celebrations.

Even Father Federico hugged all the women, with such vigour and joy that under different circumstances it would have caused murmurs of disapproval from the more devout. Some of the women felt ashamed, because the only thing they regretted about the end of the rain was that they'd no longer see his legs – he had such a fine pair. And Joseph the Carpenter, who hadn't been back to church since the death of his daughter Gracia, not even when the weather was at its hottest, went to give thanks to God and to the Pink Virgin of Navidad – but he wouldn't make it up with his ex-relative, Saint Joseph, no way.

And although most villagers had lost their crops, their homes, their furniture, their businesses, their farms, the little they owned, that day, when the rain stopped, was the happiest day of their lives.

Amadeo the Idiot was wild with joy. He rang the bells in such a frenzy that his hands ended up raw and bleeding, and Father Federico had to get him out of the bell tower. But Amadeo didn't feel the pain, because that day the villagers felt nothing but joy. All except for Federico the donkey, who just went about his business as usual. Now he was shaking his ears, warning of impending bad weather, but the weather had never been as splendid as that day. In Navidad, legends obviously didn't come true: what with the one about the donkey, who never got it right about the weather, and the one about the Rainbow, which they preferred to keep quiet about, they'd had more than ample proof. Thank goodness their promises seemed to get better results.

Now that he'd made it up with his daughter, Juan Quintana felt like the luckiest man alive. He let the children ring the cow-bell and gave all his neighbours free drinks, something which he hadn't even done on his wedding day. They all had a drink, except Pedro the Blind Man, who had three: the one he had every day as usual, the one he had to celebrate and the one he dropped on the floor due to his customary clumsiness. Inspired by the alcohol, he started saying he could see colours again, but nobody took any notice of him because he claimed Juan Quintana was wearing a black shirt and Joseph the Carpenter a blue one – he wasn't even close, they were both wearing white shirts. Even Father Federico had a little glass of wine to celebrate, and it must have gone to his head because he wanted to hug all the women in the tavern. Priests are only human after all.

For the first time Berta saw her father kiss her mother on the mouth. She smiled and shut her eyes and imagined herself kissing Jonas. And when she went to bed, Roberta Anaya felt so happy she let Juan Quintana suck her left breast even though it wasn't a Sunday or a holiday: the truth is they had a lot of days to make up.

The mayor, Feliciano the Saint, was the most subdued. First because the village had been totally destroyed by the rain: 'Now what are we going to do? We'll have to start all over again.' And second, because Margarita, in her euphoria, was talking more than ever, and so fast, that you could hardly understand her: 'It's-stoppedrainingatlast, Icouldn'ttakeitanymore,butwhat'sto bedone, we'llhavetoworkveryhardbutwe'llmanage.You'llsee Feliciano, I'llhelpyou, rememberwe'remarriedforbetterfor-worse, blah,blah.'

That night lots of couples must have made love because nine months later four babies were born around the same time, something that had never happened before in Navidad. Three of them were girls and all three were named Rosa in honour of the Pink Virgin, and somebody suggested that the boy be named Federico because the priest had helped so much. But the parents didn't want their son to have the same name as the donkey, who'd turned out to be a complete ass, and in the end they decided to call the child Macario.

That night Berta La Larga couldn't sleep, wondering if Jonas was alive. Juan Quintana went to her room to say good night, and he sat beside her, and told her how much he loved her. He must have noticed she was sad and he asked what the matter was, and she said: 'Nothing.' She couldn't tell her father she was in love: her love for Jonas created a deep rift between them. But that night Berta La Larga asked him if she could go back to work in the tavern. Now that they were close again, Juan Quintana said yes. He wouldn't upset his daughter again for anything in the world. Berta hugged him: 'You're the best father in the world.' Juan Quintana felt immensely happy and proud that his daughter was so keen to work in the tavern: he was sure the child's obsession with keeping the tavern porch so clean was to attract more customers, something she'd no doubt inherited from him.

Lluvia

.
.
.
.
.
.
.
.
.
.
.
.
.
.
.
.

Navidad

Literary rain over Navidad

The following day many villagers awoke thinking they must have dreamed that the rain had stopped, but when they went outside the sky was still blue with a radiant sun smiling over it. They were still hung over from all the celebrating, but the first thing they did was have a collection, and for once, everybody contributed as much as they could. Only Alberto the Baker complained, declaring that the promise was a load of nonsense, but when he saw his neighbours weren't looking too pleased with him, he decided to keep quiet. Several men went to the capital to buy metres and metres of pink fabric. They also purchased pink dye – for dyeing shoes and leather goods – in such large quantities that the shopkeepers stared at them oddly, because the villagers gave no explanation.

While Navidad prepared to keep its promise, Berta La Larga went to the outskirts of the village to wait for Jonas. She crouched behind some bushes, and the seconds seemed like hours and the hours like centuries: what if Jonas didn't appear, what if he'd been swallowed up by the water? Eventually, Jonas did appear but the road must have been very bad because his bicycle was covered in mud and he was over two hours late. When Berta heard the bicycle, she emerged from her hiding place. Her heart was beating so hard it was louder than her own footsteps as she stepped towards him, and they stared at each other.

Thanks to the rain, which had kept them apart for several weeks, they now felt closer than ever and they spoke to each other for the first time. They had so much to say, so much love to share. Berta was the first to speak, but she was so nervous she couldn't get the words out, and she stammered so much that even Amadeo the Idiot would have done better. She said: 'I 1-1-1-1-love you.' And Jonas stammered back: 'I 1-1-1-1-love you.'

So that nobody should see them, Berta took Jonas by the hand and led him to the Corner of Heaven. The fire Berta felt when she touched him before had now turned into a love as pure as her promise. Jonas came close and embraced her with all his might, and it was wonderful. But the embrace lasted only a few seconds, because Berta La Larga remembered her promise, and quickly moved away. Jonas didn't understand, and now she suddenly became all sad and covered her face with her hands. 'I'm sorry,' said Berta. Luckily she had recovered the power of speech and told him about her promise. That day, Jonas felt immensely happy just to see her, and he said they'd keep the promise, he'd have agreed to anything, just being with her was enough. On hearing this Berta felt very proud of him. To thank him for being so understanding she embraced him once more, and again disengaged herself in a flash, and she said they could get married as soon as she was eighteen. The truth is, Jonas was a little disappointed but, as we all know, nothing's perfect, not even love. They went for a walk, hand in hand, and Jonas told her it had rained a lot in Ponsa, though not as much as in Navidad, and on several occasions he'd tried to come and see her, but it was impossible because the road was more like a river than a road, and Jonas said he too had wanted to die. But now they were alive, they felt more alive than they'd ever been, and they loved each other, and they had their whole lives before them.

After her meeting with Jonas, Berta ran back to the tavern. She was very late, but luckily Juan Quintana had gone to the capital with the men to buy pink dye and pink fabric. Before she started sweeping, she went to her mother and hugged her and said: 'You're the best mother in the world.' Roberta understood: she'd seen Jonas. In the space of a few hours Berta had gone from being the unhappiest woman in the world to being the happiest woman in the entire universe: 'Isn't life marvellous? Isn't sweeping wonderful?' Jonas came to deliver the post shortly afterwards, and when he saw the village, he was shocked by the state it was in: there was mud everywhere. That day Roberta Anaya collected the post and she said to the postman: 'Take care of her, she's still a child.' Jonas was stunned, but not exactly by her words: it was her breasts, he'd never seen them so close up. Shame her daughter's weren't the same.

While Berta could think of nothing but Jonas, the villagers' only thought was rebuilding the village. Using the pink fabric, the women sewed for whole days and nights and made all kinds of garments. They also made the most of the clothes they already had and placed them in huge vats so they could be dyed. They poured in the dye and dipped all their light-coloured clothes in the pink solution, because they realized there was no way they'd be able to dye dark clothes. They also dyed leather for making shoes and painted the shoes they already owned pink. At first the women gathered outside the church to work, but Margarita Cifuentes wouldn't stop talking, so they decided to sew at home so they wouldn't have to listen to her. Berta helped her mother – not much though, because since seeing Jonas she was in more of a daze than ever – and told her how much she loved him, and that one day they'd get married, and she felt so light-headed that she pricked herself with her needle several times, and when she saw the blood, she said even that seemed beautiful to her. But her mother warned her that Juan Quintana would never give his approval: 'The boy's from Ponsa, it would give your father the shock of his life.' She didn't press her point too hard because she'd never seen Berta so happy, although she told her again to be very careful: 'Men are animals.' Berta thought of her promise but she didn't say anything because it was a secret between her, Jonas and God, although she reassured her mother: 'Don't worry, mother, we won't do anything bad.'

While Berta, her mother and all the women of Navidad sewed and dyed clothes, the men got on with rebuilding their houses, their farms, their furniture, their shops. They helped one another, and they had never been so mutually supportive. Even Alberto the Baker, who always did his own thing, joined in without complaining, and, incredibly, he even smiled on several occasions. And thank goodness for Amadeo the Idiot: with his great strength, he helped everyone put things back in their place, moving furniture and animals – he'd never had so many tips, which made Juan Quintana very envious. Father Federico wanted to help too, and the women immediately offered him clothes to change into so he wouldn't spoil his cassock. They gave him shorts, assuring him they'd be more comfortable for working in, but really they just wanted to see his legs. The priest, naturally, wasn't too happy about showing his legs, but he put on the shorts without complaining, because it had been very thoughtful of them.

Starting from the week after the floods, Jonas arranged things so he could see Berta La Larga at weekends, as well as on the days he brought the post. Berta and Jonas saw each other not only on Mondays, Wednesdays and Fridays, but also on Saturdays and Sundays, so now there were only two days that Berta hated: Tuesdays and Thursdays. They met at the Corner of Heaven, where they spent hours and hours staring up at the blue sky, and Berta showed him how to play the cloud game: 'Look at that cloud up there, it looks like a face.' But Jonas proved to have very little imagination: 'I can't see a face. Where can you see a face?' Berta showed him where the eyes and mouth were. 'Now I see it.' 'I can see a couple kissing.' 'Where?' 'Now I can see a car.' 'Where?' Poor Jonas couldn't see anything, but Berta didn't care that he had such a poor imagination, because she loved him: nothing's perfect, not even love. Jonas desired her violently, but she would only let him kiss her gently and caress her – in certain places. Ears were allowed, so was her nose, but breasts were out of the question; legs, lower only, arms, every bit of them. But Berta was only human too, she felt desire as well, and she was scared of forgetting her promise, so she decided to tie a pink ribbon round her wrist to remind her.

A week and a half after it stopped raining, everything was ready for the whole village to get dressed in pink the following day. The women brought all the clothes to the church and distributed them amongst the families. Pink shoes, pink jumpers, pink socks, pink trousers, pink waistcoats, pink girdles, pink tights, pink skirts, pink blouses, pink hats, pink handkerchiefs, pink ties. The clothes looked funny all together, like a big pink blob, and while the men laughed at the thought of themselves wearing pink, the women said very seriously: 'You can laugh all you want, but we have to keep the promise.'

There was a great deal of discussion about whether underwear had to be pink too, and they decided in the end that it didn't, because the men flatly refused – it was bad enough wearing pink outer garments – and the discussion ended when someone said very wisely that one didn't go out in one's underwear and at home one could do as one pleased. The only villager forced to wear pink underwear was Pedro the Blind Man, because his underpants were all different colours, and they were always on show, because his flies were always undone. At first he refused, because he'd heard that pink was a very feminine colour. He promised he'd never leave his flies undone again, but nobody believed him. The women convinced him in the end, saying it was a sign of character for a man to wear pink underpants.

They also summoned Father Federico and told him he had to change his cassock; the women had made him a pink one. Father Federico laughed at his parishioners' absurd suggestion. He'd agreed to wear the shorts, but there was no way they were going to get him into a pink cassock. But they were so insistent that he decided to consult the ecclesiastical authorities in the capital. The bishop, when he met Father Federico, thought the young priest must have been drinking or maybe he'd had some sort of breakdown, it happened to all of them at some stage, particularly when they were sent to lost villages like Navidad. Luckily for him, the bishop was in an excellent mood that day and decided to forget their meeting. And after some hesitation, the parishioners decided that he could be the only villager not to wear pink, taking into account that he was the best priest they'd had for a long time, and anyway better the devil you know.

Anatomy of one of Father Federico's attractive legs

Juan Quintana put on the clothes Roberta Anaya had left him ready on a chair as usual: trousers, shirt and shoes, this time all pink. When his wife saw him she couldn't help laughing. Nor could his daughter when she saw him. The truth is, he really did look ridiculous dressed from head to toe in pink. Juan Quintana realized he looked absurd and refused to go out like that. While he was undressing, Roberta Anaya (also dressed in pink, but being a woman she didn't look any different from normal) reminded him of the promise and the consequences if they didn't keep it, and Juan Quintana put all the pink clothes back on again.

The same happened in nearly every family: the men thought they looked ridiculous dressed in pink. So that day, Roberta opened the tavern, as Juan Quintana refused to leave the house, and there were hardly any customers because, like Juan

Quintana, most of the men wouldn't leave home – the most they would do was peep cautiously from their windows. The older ones were the most reluctant to wear pink, principally because of its feminine connotations. But it was Alberto the Baker who took it worst: when he saw himself all in pink he started to curse old Inés for having made the promise; when they heard, the women pounced on him furiously: 'How could you say such a thing? We'd have drowned if it hadn't been for her.' When he saw how cross they were, he tried to appease them, saying she could at least have picked a different colour.

As most of the men wouldn't leave their houses, the women helped one another drag their husbands out into the street. It took five women, for instance, to get Joseph the Carpenter out. Being beefier and grumpier, Alberto the Baker put up more of a fight, and Remedios had to get seven women to help her. On the other hand, it took just Margarita Cifuentes to get the mayor, Feliciano the Saint, out of the house: he'd rather look ridiculous wearing pink in public than put up with her. Juan Quintana went down to the tavern when he saw other men walking around the village, but he did so mainly because he was worried he'd lose customers. Pedro the Blind Man went out in green and black, as he couldn't see what he was wearing, so they had to go to his house and get rid of all the clothes of different colours, and replace them with pink ones. Some of the children lost all respect for their parents when they saw them dressed in pink. Amadeo the Idiot couldn't help laughing, and his father walloped him more than once because all this pink business was making him see red.

Within a week, all the inhabitants were dressed in a single colour: pink. They gradually got used to it. As Remedios said: 'There's no remedy.' At first, they stared at each other oddly, the whispers were constant. Some just couldn't help smiling, and it caused several brawls, which the women quickly broke up. The men told Pedro the Blind Man he was very lucky he couldn't see what he looked like in pink. 'And do up your flies.'

After two weeks, there remained only one villager who still hadn't appeared in public: Dolores the Grocer's husband, Tomas, who proved to be more stubborn than Federico the donkey. He stayed indoors, telling Dolores he'd rather die than go out dressed all in pink: he stopped farming his land and took to drink. Dolores was in despair and she asked for help. Several men, amongst them Juan Quintana, came to her house, but nothing doing, Tomas would lock himself in the toilet whenever he heard approaching footsteps. Father Federico went to see him as well but Tomas said to him: 'You're not wearing pink, so I'm not going to either.' In an attack of hysteria, Dolores set fire to the house, to force him out, but even the flames wouldn't make him change his mind: Tomas didn't turn a hair, he sat in the dining room and waited. Dolores tried to drag him from his chair, but all in vain. And he died, proving that he was a man of his word, because he swore he'd rather die than wear pink. And although somebody said they should put him in a pink shroud, Dolores flatly refused: 'Show some respect for the dead.' In order to keep the promise, they managed to convince the widow to have him laid out naked in his coffin, covering him with a couple of sheets, first a white one, then a pink one. They wrapped the pink one round him just before the coffin was closed so Dolores didn't see, and more than one person was thinking, If only Margarita Cifuentes had died in the fire, because with all the goings-on in the village, she was talking more than ever, which was really saying something.

If anyone was in tune with the colour of the village, it was Berta. She viewed the world through rose-tinted spectacles, and when Jonas saw her dressed in pink, he was delighted, she looked lovelier than ever. Berta was so happy she said it all seemed like a wonderful dream, and he pinched her, as if to wake her up – it was a good excuse to touch her. She moved away, saying: 'Remember the promise.'

In the Corner of Heaven, Jonas and Berta gradually got to know each other, and Berta asked her beloved why he was called Jonas, she'd never heard the name before. He explained it was because his parents used to meet in the Cave of the Whale, so called because the entrance resembled a cetacean's mouth. It was a little way from Ponsa and you had to climb a crag to reach it.

Jonas became sad as he told her the story and, when she heard it, Berta understood why he'd never recounted it to her in his letters: he didn't want to make her sad. Jonas's father was a travelling salesman, and he met Jonas's mother on one of his trips. They fell in love, but theirs was an impossible love because he was already married. They'd meet at the Cave of the Whale, and loved each other in secret: they planned to run off together, but then Jonas's mother became pregnant, and the salesman, when he found out, disappeared for ever. His mother died in childbirth, but before she died she said she wanted her son to be called Jonas, after the prophet in the Bible, because he was conceived in the Cave of the Whale. And Enriqueta, Jonas's aunt, took him in and treated him like a son. Berta was moved by the story, and thought how lucky she was to have a father like Juan Quintana who loved her so much, and when he came to accept her relationship with Jonas, he'd be the best father in the world. Berta said she'd like to see the Cave of the Whale one day. Jonas explained that it wasn't very large but it was very comfortable, cool in summer and warm in winter, and lovers' words of love echoed around the cave, and there was no danger of being seen, because from inside the cave you could hear anyone approaching. They agreed to go the following week, but Berta, feeling the pink ribbon round her wrist, remembered the promise, and mentioned it to Jonas. As usual he was understanding; he was beginning to seem like a bit of a saint. But saints aren't made of stone. He felt a strong desire to undress her, touch her breasts, and when he felt the animal inside him stirring, he moved away from her, made any old excuse to go for a walk, and didn't come back until it had calmed down. And they found parting terribly painful, they just wanted to see each other again.

When Jonas walked into the village after his meeting with Berta, and saw them all dressed in pink, he couldn't believe his eyes, even though Berta had told him about the promise the whole village had made. First he saw a man dressed in pink, then an entire family, then another man. He thought he must be dreaming, or maybe his breakfast hadn't agreed with him – he had eaten rather a lot that morning. He shook his head, as if to wake himself up, but they were still wearing pink. When Jonas saw Juan Quintana, he found it terribly difficult not to laugh, particularly when he thought that this ridiculous man would one day be his father-in-law. He handed him the post more quickly than usual and nearly burst out laughing.

That day, Jonas returned to Ponsa still amazed by what he'd seen. He told his aunt Enriqueta all about it. At first she didn't believe him, but then she thought, the boy didn't talk much, so when he did he must have good reason. And in turn Jonas's aunt told all her neighbours and the news soon spread.

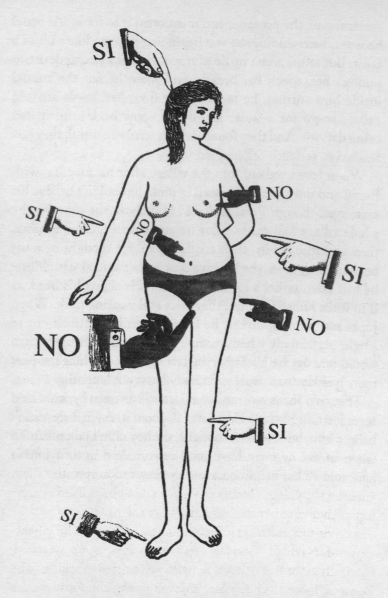

The only parts of Berta's body that Jonas can touch
after the promise

The news soon spread that there was a village where everyone wore pink, and Navidad – now becoming a great curiosity in the region – came to be known as the Pink Village. Sightseers began to arrive, at first from nearby villages, then from further afield. It was undoubtedly the Ponsans who felt the greatest curiosity, and although the inhabitants of Navidad gave them a cold reception they couldn't very well stop them entering the village – not that they wouldn't have liked to try – just as they couldn't stop flies from getting in.

The visitors' initial reaction was surprise. At first the inhabitants of Navidad found it very annoying to be watched, especially since the visitors' remarks were often mocking. The Ponsans, more than anyone, enjoyed seeing the most macho men wearing pink, and they laughed at them, but they were discreet about it because they were outnumbered. Amadeo the

Idiot didn't take kindly to being laughed at, so he grabbed one of them by the lapels, but things didn't go any further, because since the floods the villagers just wanted a quiet life. It took three men to get Amadeo the Idiot off the Ponsan, and to avoid further trouble, they put a sign at the entrance to the village which read: 'Please respect the manner of dress of the inhabitants of Navidad.'

It was actually very funny to see old people dressed in pink sitting on their porches, women in pink having a lunch-time gossip, a large pink mass of children playing in the school yard, and they made up a song that they sang during breaks, which soon became famous.

> Thank you Pink Virgin,
> you saved us from the flood.
> Thank you Pink Virgin
> for bringing back the sun,
> Now we're really in the pink,
> Thank you Pink Virgin,
> you saved us from the flood.

Just to be on the safe side, only the children with the best voices were allowed to sing it, because they were afraid a bad voice might annoy God. Doña Lucia no longer sang: every night someone made sure to dissolve a sleeping pill in her bedtime glass of milk, so she slept straight through the night, and she must have slept very deeply because, in the quiet of the night, you could hear her snoring throughout the village, but there was absolutely no doubt that it was preferable to her singing.

Juan Quintana was enjoying prosperity such as he'd never known before. The tavern couldn't cope with all the customers, it was filled with tourists every day and the cowbell was constantly ringing because of all the tips. The tourists turned out to be more generous than the villagers, although that wasn't saying much. From then on, the spare room was always taken, and because Juan Quintana was incapable of turning a customer away, when they needed more than one room, he moved into his daughter's room with his wife and all three of them slept together. Poor Roberta Anaya now had to work harder than ever and, on top of not having the sewing room she'd always dreamed of, she'd even lost her own bedroom.

So much money poured into the village that Juan Quintana earned more in a month than he used to in a whole year, and with the money earned over those days, together with a loan granted by the mayor Feliciano the Saint, he decided to build a hotel for all the visitors. With the help of Joseph the Carpenter and Amadeo the Idiot, he worked day and night, and between the three of them they finished the hotel in record time; they had to hurry, more visitors were arriving all the time. In his obsession to attract customers, he decided to paint it pink inside and out. He had all the furniture painted pink, and all the sheets, curtains, carpets and towels dyed pink too.

The hotel was built in only two weeks, and then Roberta Anaya got her bedroom back and had the spare room to herself as well. She made it into a sewing room, but now that she had what she'd always dreamed of, she didn't have time to use it because, while Juan Quintana ran the hotel, Roberta Anaya had to take charge of the tavern. And Juan Quintana built himself a new bathroom because the child was having stomach trouble again, but he didn't have time to enjoy it either. As Juan Quintana thought painting the hotel pink had been a brainwave, he decided to paint the tavern pink too. If great-grandfather had been alive . . . but better leave him where he was: Juan Quintana even painted the wooden leg pink and the tavern became known as The Pink Pirate.

Juan Quintana had so much work he had to take on an

employee, the nephew of the mayor; Feliciano the Saint hadn't granted him the loan for nothing. They boy was totally inept. But Juan Quintana was so busy that he didn't have time to worry about it, or about whether his daughter had her eye on some man – he had even less time to go to the lovers' tree to check, though it was more obvious than ever that the child was in love. By the end of the day he was so exhausted that on more than one holiday he fell asleep on Roberta's left breast, and she had to move his head to one side and lay it on the pillow. 'You're going to work yourself into the ground. Good night.' It was lucky for Berta La Larga that her father was so busy: she could meet her beloved without arousing his suspicions, and only Roberta Anaya knew: 'I'm meeting Jonas.'

Juan Quintana was so ambitious he wanted even more customers, and he had an idea that they all applauded: he suggested to the villagers that all the houses in Navidad should be painted pink, and all the cars and signs too. Within a month, almost all the houses in the village were pink, and even the church was pink, despite Father Federico's objections. As his parishioners put so much pressure on him, he said he'd consult the ecclesiastical authorities, but this time the villagers were firm, remembering what happened with the cassock: 'Pink is the colour of our Virgin, after all.'

Roses, geraniums and other pink flowers gradually appeared on all the balconies; the washing lines were hung with pink clothes, and when the sun shone at its brightest, there was a pink glare that almost damaged your eyes, and from the mountain tops, amongst the greenery, a large pink patch could be seen.

Visitors kept on arriving from further and further afield, particularly from the capital. Many of them had cameras and took so many photos of the inhabitants of Navidad that they found it rather trying, and decided by a great majority that the tourists should pay every time they wanted to immortalize them in a photograph. This meant that the wiliest villagers dressed in the most extravagant fashion in order to attract the tourists' cameras. One villager became famous for wearing a pink top hat almost three feet high; another dyed his dog pink. The dog, by the way, didn't take to his new colour. The poor animal knew nothing of promises, fame or money, and he became terribly depressed – he must have thought humans were very strange: 'Pigs are so lucky, they're already pink, and hens are lucky because their feathers are impossible to dye, and cows are too busy producing milk.' As a result of the dye, he lost his sense of smell: 'It's a dog's life.' And because he also had poor eyesight, being very old, he ate an ember, mistaking it for raw meat, and died. And somebody thought: If only Margarita Cifuentes had swallowed the ember.

They painted Federico the donkey pink too, and stood him at the entrance to he village as an advert, as he was obviously no good at predicting anything. He was constantly shaking his ears now, a sign of impending bad weather, when it had never been so good, the silly ass.

While the village prospered, the love between Berta and Jonas grew as quickly as they had as children. They met at the Corner of Heaven and spent hours and hours holding hands, and they never tired of being together. Berta said their love would be perfect if only her father approved of the relationship, and Jonas said that if he didn't, they'd leave and go far away. 'I can't do that. After you, I love my parents more than anyone in the world.' Jonas, for his part, thought their love would be perfect if they could do more than just kiss and cuddle innocently. His desire to possess her increased day by day. And they told each other almost everything, even the most insignificant details of their lives; because of the promise they couldn't do much else really. Luckily for Jonas, the sky was so clear at that time that they couldn't play the cloud game very often. Jonas was starting to get really bored with it, particularly when they could have been doing much more interesting things. Then his eyes were drawn to her breasts and, unintentionally, he remembered Roberta Anaya's breasts, and he really ought not to compare.

It was obvious that Berta was much more concerned with keeping the promise than Jonas. But now she was getting to know him, Berta had her own tricks for cooling her beloved's ardour: she only allowed him to kiss her seven times when they first met, because she'd noticed that after the eighth kiss Jonas's hands started wandering. Another trick she'd learned from her mother was to say she had a headache. It was something Roberta resorted to when her father became excessively amorous on the wrong days. Which hadn't occurred, by the way, since Juan Quintana had got so busy. And like her mother, Berta gave her man a reward on Sundays and holidays. Not her left breast, because of the promise, but a kiss with tongues. But only one, because Jonas got all fired up.

And it must be said that, in spite of everything, Jonas preferred to have her like that – not having her – than to lose her. He loved her deeply, and anyway there was only a year to go until Berta was eighteen, and then they'd get married. God bless the day Berta La Larga turned eighteen.

With all those customers Juan Quintana was so happy that Berta La Larga asked her mother whether now was a good time to tell him she was in love with Jonas. She spent several days rehearsing what she'd say: 'Daddy, I love you very much, and if you really love me, you'll understand that I have a right to fall in love and be happy.' Juan Quintana was so busy that it was almost a week before Berta La Larga managed to get her father on his own, and she'd never been so nervous in all her life. She knew her happiness depended on the words she was about to say, and she had to hide her hands so her father wouldn't see they were trembling. But in the end all she managed to get out was 'Daddy, I love you very much', because Juan Quintana interrupted and answered: 'I love you very much too, but now I've got to get back to work.' There was no way of getting through to him, because all he ever thought about was his damned hotel, and his blasted customers and how to attract more of them, but he had plenty of time to tell her about his new scheme – which was to offer his customers a pink menu: prawns, salmon, salad with a pink dressing, and strawberries for dessert. He was so obsessed with everything being pink that there was a bout of food poisoning because of all the food colouring. Several customers threw up everything they'd eaten, and their vomit was a violent pink. It looked so unpleasant that Juan Quintana almost threw up himself when he saw it. To fend off any complaints, he decided to invite the victims to spend a free night at the hotel.

Despite several minor incidents, such as the one mentioned above, the village became a prosperous place, and not only for Juan Quintana. They had to build two new hotels and several bars and restaurants. With more houses being built, Joseph the Carpenter had more work, since most of them were made of wood, and he also sold all kinds of furniture painted pink. It meant he could give all his children jobs, and with the money he saved he built the other hotel in the village. This made Juan Quintana angry, because Joseph the Carpenter had copied everything Juan Quintana had done, even down to the pink decor. Villagers who made their living farming the land or breeding cattle also thrived, since most of the visitors after their long journey arrived hungry and needed to eat. The only petrol pump in the village, which was hardly used before because there were so few cars in Navidad, became a petrol station, because cars had to be fed too, with petrol for the return journey.

Someone suggested that the petrol station should be pink, and the idea was very popular at first but, after the food poisoning cases, it was rejected.

With all the hustle and bustle, Dolores got over her husband's death. In the shop there was always some customer to be served, tourists, mainly from the capital, who came to her shop to stock up, because her prices were much more reasonable than those in the capital, and now she was thinking of moving to larger premises where she'd have plenty of room for her merchandise. The hairdresser had never had so much business, because now that the women of the village were photographed so often they wanted to look nice in the pictures, and at first some of them dyed their hair pink. The only problem was that afterwards, when they washed their hair, all the dye came out, and one woman, a slightly over-anxious type, nearly died as a result, because when she had a bath she saw all this pink liquid and she thought it was blood: she was so scared she jumped out of the bath and slipped, nearly cracking her skull open. Fortunately she only sprained her wrist which had to be put in a plaster cast – painted pink, naturally. And somebody thought, if only Margarita Cifuentes had had an accident in the bath and cracked her skull open. And the barber too was overjoyed: the men had never frequented his premises so often. They wanted to look handsome so they could flirt with the female tourists, and it has to be said, they were far more attractive than the women of Navidad, particularly the ones from the capital who were very slim, neat and smartly turned out.

Acting on an idea given to him by Juan Quintana, Alberto the Baker invented a pink cake, made with strawberries. It proved very popular with the visitors and with the villagers themselves, because it was delicious. Amadeo the Idiot liked it the most, and Alberto the Baker had to keep the pink cakes under lock and key, or the boy would eat them all. Even Pedro the Blind Man did well, because now that there were so many tourists he went begging in the street. He'd never had so much money. Some of the female visitors were shocked when they saw his flies open, and he'd say: 'If you want me to do them up, give me some money.' And he let his hands wander; he'd never touched so many bottoms. 'You disgusting man.' But they forgave him, because he was blind. And when Juan Quintana found out that Pedro the Blind Man was making such a good living, he stopped giving him free drinks: he could jolly well pay for them, and what a coincidence, now that Pedro the Blind Man had to buy his own drinks, he never dropped a single one on the floor.

Margarita Cifuentes set up a boutique where she sold only pink clothes. The mayor encouraged her because he saw it as a way of avoiding her incessant chatter. She went to the capital to buy her stock, also with the encouragement of the mayor, who wanted her as far away as possible. He urged her to spend a few days in the capital, where she had family: 'Seeing as you're there, darling, why don't you make the most of it and go and visit them.' The boutique was a great success, nearly everyone who went in bought a piece of clothing. Anything, as long as they didn't have to listen to her.

New jobs were created: some villagers worked as tourist guides, and others, like the Montalbo brothers, who'd farmed the mayor Feliciano the Saint's land before the flood, and who'd always wanted to go into show business, now put on puppet shows telling the story of the Pink Village, and they made a puppet of Father Federico and a puppet of old Inés who made the promise, and the climax of the story was when the sun came out after all the rain. For the first few shows, Amadeo the Idiot helped with the rain effect, by standing on a chair and flinging rice over the little theatre. But he did it with such force that he almost damaged the puppets, and then there was an invasion of ants who turned up to feast on the grains of rice that were lying all over the floor. Amadeo the Idiot was fired, to his great disappointment because he'd really enjoyed himself.

The Montalbo brothers proved to be very creative: they added new ideas to the show so that people coming to see it for a second time wouldn't get bored. They told the story of the founding of Navidad and the legend of the Rainbow, but now they linked it more closely to the colour of the village. They said the first settlers had seen a Rainbow, but it was entirely pink. Luckily for Berta, who was so shy she'd have died of shame, they didn't mention that she was the first baby to be born under the Rainbow, as it would no doubt have been a great disappointment to the audience. In the Montalbo brothers' new version, the Pink Rainbow was the great premonition of the promise the villagers would make to the Pink Virgin three hundred years later.

And the mayor Feliciano the Saint was applauded when he decided that a stretch of the road leading to Navidad should be repaired. And Amadeo the Idiot had never been so busy, as he declared his love to all the girls who visited Navidad: 'I l-l-l-love you.' But they didn't take any notice of him either.

Jonas had never had so much post to deliver to Navidad. Many of the letters were from tourists requesting information, and mayor Feliciano didn't have time to answer them so he asked his wife to help him. Margarita Cifuentes had never been so busy in her life; when she shut the boutique, she had to spend time reading all the letters, and she didn't even feel like talking. By the end of the day she was so exhausted that she fell asleep almost instantly. The mayor Feliciano was delighted with the silence, but his happiness was short-lived because soon after those days of blissful tranquillity there was a new development: Margarita Cifuentes began talking in her sleep, and she talked and she talked, listing in detail the contents of all the letters and the sales at the boutique and thousands of other things. To make matters even worse, Margarita Cifuentes got hold of a catalogue so she could order her stock without having to go to the capital.

And amongst all the letters they received, there was one that brought great joy: the National Cartography Department sent them a new map of the region on which Navidad appeared in capital letters, and beneath the name it said: 'The Pink Village, tourist attraction.' It was highly moving, but it was nothing compared to the commotion when they saw that the name of Ponsa appeared in smaller letters than Navidad.

Happy Navidad.

Donkey painted pink

Federico the donkey welcomes you to the village of Navidad

During that period an albino girl was born in the village whom they called the pink child. She was one of the children conceived the night of the promise. And the name her parents decided to give her in honour of the Virgin, if she was a girl, could not have suited her better: Rosa. Despite the doctor's assurances that she was simply an albino, her skin was so pink that many villagers believed it was another of the Pink Virgin's miracles. Believing that the baby would bring them health and prosperity, they asked the mother if they could touch her. If tourists wanted to touch her they had to pay a sum equivalent to three photos.

The village church became a place of pilgrimage. Old Inés proudly explained the story and miracle of the Pink Virgin who'd saved the village of Navidad from the flood. People came from far afield to request a miracle, and, it has to be said, their faith was so strong that the Virgin really ought to have granted their requests. When Pedro the Blind Man found out that people were asking the Pink Virgin to perform miracles, he went to beg her to give him back his sight: what he most wanted was to be able to see women's bottoms. But as he was clumsy as well as blind, he tripped on a pew as he entered the church, and fell over, and had the bad luck to break his leg. That was how Pedro came to the church blind and hoping to be cured, and came out blind and crippled and in a foul temper that lasted several weeks.

Father Federico was proud of his church, which was so busy that even he couldn't believe it. He never tired of thanking God in Heaven, who'd been the cause of it all, and his only cross to bear was Margarita Cifuentes. In addition to telling him about her sins, and recipes and the fashion in the capital, she now told him about each and every one of the tourists who came to the village.

Three months after the miracle of the Pink Virgin, Father Federico had had a visit from the ecclesiastical authorities. The mayor Feliciano the Saint and his wife Margarita Cifuentes also came out to receive them, and of course it was she who explained all about the divine manifestation, with such fervour and, above all, in such detail that they were still there at nightfall. By then, the archbishop had a splitting headache and couldn't take any more, even though he'd heard only half the story, so he said he had to return to the capital and promised he'd inform the Vatican so they could make the relevant enquiries. Anything, as long as he didn't have to go on listening to that woman.

The visitors left such generous sums in the collection box that there was enough to repair the village clock, a very expensive operation as two repair men had to be called from the capital. They all wanted to be present at the historic moment when the clock was put into operation, and in honour of the time at which the clock stopped thirty-one years ago, they decided to call it the Ten Past Seven clock. People no longer had an excuse for being late for church, so those who didn't want to go to Mass used the hoards of tourists as an excuse, because inevitably, it was on Sundays and holidays that there were the most visitors: 'We can't just ignore them, can we?' And they sent pink flowers to church instead.

The inhabitants of Navidad knew that they owed their unexpected prosperity to the Pink Virgin, and they showed their gratitude by offering up pink flowers and daily prayers, and by faithfully keeping their promise: even brides wore pink on their wedding day, and it also became the colour of mourning, despite the objections of the old people, who were told that they should wear black in their hearts. Roberta Anaya and many other mothers in Navidad were deeply disappointed that brides had to wear pink, as they'd always dreamed of their daughters marrying in white, just as they, their mothers, their grandmothers and all previous generations had done, and many asked what was the point of having kept their wedding dresses so carefully for their daughters to wear. But, to be honest, Roberta Anaya had got over that particular disappointment years ago – what with her daughter's height and her own ample bosom, she knew she'd have to make Berta a new wedding dress when the time came.

It was at that time that Berta La Larga and Jonas El Largo became engaged in the right and proper fashion, with God as their witness: the two lovers were gazing up at the clouds when Berta saw one shaped like a ring and pointed it out to her beloved. It was so well defined that even he could see it perfectly. He remained deep in thought for a few moments, then took his beloved's hand and raised it and asked her to hold out her ring finger, and said that the ring in the sky would be their engagement ring, and Jonas did the same himself: he raised his hand and held out his ring finger, and there were tears of joy in Berta's eyes. She was so happy she let Jonas give her the regulation seven kisses plus an extra one, even though it was neither a Sunday nor a holiday. And by the eighth kiss Jonas was holding her so tight that for the first time Berta had real difficulty getting him to let go. When she managed it at last, Jonas raised his voice, saying he was fed up with the damned promise. Fortunately, Jonas regretted what he'd said and done, begging forgiveness. And he really meant it, because he didn't want to lose her. And God bless the day of Berta's eighteenth birthday.

But not all was happiness in Navidad, mainly because of money, which not everyone knew how to handle. The Montalbo brothers, who'd always been very close, almost killed each other, and all because the elder brother was cheating the younger one out of money, and when the younger one found out, he was furious. Now they were known as Cain and Abel, and each put on his own show, but they both lost out because the new shows they put on separately weren't nearly as good.

Nor did the massive influx of tourists benefit everyone – Margarita Cifuentes, for instance: the mayor Feliciano the Saint fell in love with a young woman from the capital, and nobody was surprised to hear that she was very quiet; by cheating on his wife, he proved that he wasn't much of a saint after all but that he was in fact rather clever, because she was a very beautiful woman. The mayor thought people wouldn't be too friendly to his mistress, but that was far from the case: they greeted the young woman as if she was a blessing from God, because when Margarita Cifuentes found out, she was struck dumb, and her last words were for the mayor: 'Get out, I don't want to see you ever again.' Feliciano moved out and went to live at Juan Quintana's hotel, and the young woman from the capital came to Navidad to see him every Saturday and Sunday. Margarita Cifuentes shut herself in her house, and hardly went out; she didn't even talk to the walls. Some people came to believe it was another miracle performed by the Pink Virgin. Unfortunately for Father Federico, she made one exception to her vow of silence: confession.

Juan Quintana still wouldn't talk to Joseph the Carpenter. He was angry that Joseph the Carpenter had copied him and built a hotel like his, but he now also accused him of being a shoddy workman: he complained that the wooden beams in The Pink Pirate hotel were of such poor quality that the whole building swayed. He wouldn't listen to Joseph the Carpenter, who said in his defence that the hotel was built in such a short time, what did he expect. Joseph the Carpenter decided he'd never set foot in the tavern again, which was a pity, they'd been such good friends. Juan Quintana also fell out with Alberto the Baker. He'd given Alberto the idea for the pink cake that proved so popular, and the least Alberto could have done was sell him cakes at a discount, but he didn't, the swine. 'I'll never give you an idea again.'

And when people came from the capital to do a feature on the Pink Village, the villagers argued over who should appear in the photos. The mayor Feliciano said he should because he was mayor; Juan Quintana said he was the one who thought of painting the village pink, and the Montalbo brothers nearly came to blows over it too. Everyone had a reason for thinking they should appear in the photos. Dolores said she had the oldest shop; Joseph the Carpenter said he'd built nearly all the houses; Alberto the Baker said he'd had to give the photographer a piece of pink cake; the man in the top hat over three feet high said he was the most original. It was all too much for the photographer, he didn't know what to say and, to everyone's surprise, he decided to take a picture of Federico the donkey.

The same thing happened when a famous painter came to Navidad. They all wanted to have their portrait done, and, once again, all the arguing was futile because in the end it turned out the painter was only interested in houses, he never painted people.

The Ponsans knew the true Rainbow legend only too well, so when they heard the new version told by the inhabitants of Navidad, they accused them of being frauds. Making sure not to be seen, they stood on the road into Navidad and informed the tourists they were being told a pack of lies. Until, that is, Father Federico caught them at it, and he must have forgotten he was a priest that day, because he sent them packing so aggressively that he surprised himself. Father Federico had been quite upset recently. Particularly by all the tourists who came to church and behaved as if they were wandering around the market: they pointed at the Pink Virgin with a total lack of respect and talked at the tops of their voices, so that the priest had to be very firm with them: 'You're in the house of the Lord.'

But it was Margarita Cifuentes, who already had quite a cross to bear, who bore the brunt of the priest's ill humour. She'd told him in great detail all about her husband's mistress and the priest had had enough. One day he lost patience and told her he had every sympathy for the mayor. Margarita Cifuentes couldn't believe her ears, and from then on she no longer went to confession either. Father Federico deeply regretted his words and went to Margarita's house, but she wouldn't listen to him. As a result, the priest spent many a sleepless night, he'd committed a grave sin and he felt so bad that, there being no other priest in the village, he decided to hear his own confession.

As they were now earning money, some villagers were able

to buy themselves cars – which they painted pink of course. Alberto the Baker bought himself one, but before he'd had it even a week, Amadeo the Idiot borrowed it without telling him and crashed it into the bakery. There were plenty of other accidents because the villagers were such inexperienced drivers. For others, like the man with the top hat three feet tall, it was a case of putting on airs and graces: he thought that because he'd had his photo taken he was more important than a film star.

It was during that time that Doña Lucia died in her sleep, and now they would no longer have to listen to her singing again, but they were sorry because, in spite of everything, she was a good person. Joseph the Carpenter made her a pink coffin, and they wrapped her in a pink shroud, and nobody complained, because she had no family, God rest her soul. For the first time in a long while, they didn't think: If only Margarita Cifuentes had died, because since she'd stopped talking she didn't bother anyone any more.

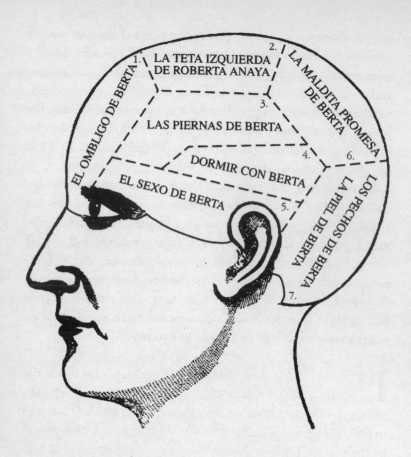

1. Berta's belly button
2. Roberta Anaya's left breast
3. Berta's legs
4. Sleeping with Berta
5. Berta's sex
6. Berta's damned promise
7. Berta's breasts
   Berta's skin

Jonas in love

If anyone couldn't stand Navidad being prosperous it was the Ponsans. All that nonsense about wearing pink. They were making a mint, and the Ponsans couldn't let it go on. They had to do something. They thought about it for days and days and by the end of it one of them said all the thinking had put him in a really black mood, and when he said 'black', one of the other Ponsans looked up at the sky and said 'blue', and nobody knew what he meant, but he'd hit on the idea they were all looking for. Glancing up at the sky again, he explained that they could be the Blue Village, and everyone applauded his idea: they sent two men to Navidad, to take detailed notes of everything they saw, making sure, above all, that the inhabitants didn't cotton on to what they were up to. And they told Jonas to take a good look round when he went to deliver the post, but Jonas didn't want any trouble and, thinking of Berta, he said he was just the postman.

The inhabitants of Ponsa waited eagerly for their spies to return, and when the two men described the huge number of tourists, they decided to act fast. They decreed that from now on all villagers had to wear blue and some houses were also to be painted blue.

As it turned out, it was quite easy for them all to wear blue. Everyone had some item of clothing in sky blue, navy blue, turquoise or dark blue, and they were allowed to wear black shoes – besides, it was really easy dying clothes navy blue, because it was such a dark colour. And as blue is suitable for both men and women, it wasn't much of a problem, except for certain mothers who liked dressing their daughters in pink. Pink was absolutely out of the question.

At first they only had a small number of visitors because Navidad was getting all the attention, so they stationed two of their most beautiful women, dressed in blue, with very plunging necklines, at the crossroads to the Pink Village. They flagged down cars and told them to come to the Blue Village, and as an added incentive they gave them a complimentary drink called the 'Heavenly Potion' – but it tasted so strongly of food colouring it was pretty foul. Miraculously, the drink didn't cause any stomach upsets, but it did give those who drank it quite a fright: their urine turned blue for several days, which wasn't funny. And poor Saint Antonio, patron saint of Ponsa, was also a victim of the times; they decided to remove him from the church and replace him with a virgin they called the Blue Virgin of Ponsa. The priest objected: you couldn't invent a Virgin just like that, but they ignored him because nothing was sacred, as long as they beat the Pink Village.

And so, very soon, the number of visitors to Navidad was reduced by half. This provoked the wrath of the villagers when they found out about the unfair competition – the cheats. Now that he had two hotels, Juan Quintana knew that if he didn't get enough customers he was sunk, and he'd go bankrupt. For the first time since they opened, over half the rooms were empty. He was so furious he started kicking the wall, and Roberta Anaya didn't know how to calm him down: 'Be careful, you don't want to end up the same as great-grandfather.' And Berta trembled as she heard her father cursing all Ponsans.

But they were all badly affected, and in the bars and restaurants the food went off because they had so few customers. Alberto the Baker didn't know what to do with all the pink cakes. Nobody went to the hairdresser or the barber: 'If there aren't any visitors there's no point in doing ourselves up.' Pedro the Blind Man hardly made any money from begging and, to cap it all, Juan Quintana didn't give him free drinks any more. The only person to do well out of it was Amadeo the Idiot because his father let him eat the strawberry cakes: 'May as well let the boy eat them rather than throw them away.'

The worse thing was that Jonas, like all his neighbours, was forced to wear blue, which actually really suited him – it matched his eyes. He objected, saying the inhabitants of Navidad would be furious when they saw him, but it didn't do any good. When he arrived with the post, he was insulted by several villagers who came out to taunt him but mainly to vent their anger, and they called him everything: bastard, son of a bitch, rat. He was the first blue-clad Ponsan they'd seen since the beginning of the conflict. Berta La Larga was sweeping the porch, and she dropped the broom in fright without thinking, and Juan Quintana came out of the tavern on hearing all the commotion. Jonas tried to defend himself, but only verbally, because he was outnumbered by fifty to one: 'Look, it's not my fault, they made me wear blue.' He wanted to glance over at Berta for moral support from his beloved but he didn't dare.

The mayor Feliciano announced that no Ponsan would be allowed to enter the village, especially if he was wearing blue, and Jonas didn't know what to do: 'I'm just the postman.' 'Not the butcher, the baker, or the candlestick-maker, not a single damned one of you.' Two men grabbed Jonas and, to teach him a lesson, they tore off his shirt and trousers. As he tried to fight them off, a few other men, including Juan Quintana, pinned him down and poor Jonas ended up in nothing but his underpants and vest, which, fortunately, were white, because if they'd been blue, God knows what would have happened. Red with shame and humiliated, Jonas had yet more insults hurled at him, stronger ones this time. Berta feared for her beloved, and without a moment's thought she turned to her father and begged him not to raise his voice against Jonas. They were all surprised to see Berta defend the young man, when normally she never said a word, and her father, when he saw the child's tearful eyes, suddenly realized that she must be in love with Jonas. Juan Quintana fell silent. His daughter had deceived him, betrayed him, when he'd given her all his love and affection. Now there was another man in her life, and a Ponsan to boot, who had stolen his daughter. The only reason Juan Quintana didn't kill him was because Roberta held on to him with all her might. Jonas walked away without a word, head bowed, in his underwear and with his bicycle tyres punctured by the children, who shouted over and over again: 'The only good Ponsan is a dead one.' And Amadeo the Idiot was speechless, because he too loved Berta, and he went home and started to bang his head against the wall.

After Jonas's departure, the men got together and declared Ponsa an enemy village. They decided by a large majority that as all Ponsans were now banned from the village, anyone who defied the ban would be killed.

Juan Quintana grabbed his daughter by the arm and dragged

her into the house: 'You've made me look a fool in front of everybody. Why did you fall in love with that bloody Ponsan, it's so humiliating.' Roberta Anaya defended her daughter: 'Leave her alone, she's just a child.' But when she saw how furious he was, Berta denied it over and over again, and she denied it so many times that Juan Quintana had a faint hope that he might have been wrong. Berta La Larga just managed to hold back her tears, made more determined by the hatred she felt for her father.

The whole village was talking about how Berta La Larga and Jonas El Largo were lovers: 'Did you see how they looked at each other? And what a blow to Juan Quintana and Roberta Anaya, they gave their daughter everything.' Amadeo the Idiot couldn't bear to hear all the talk, and he thought of his beloved Berta La Larga: 'It's not true, they can't be in love.' He knocked on the door at the Quintanas' house to talk to Berta, and from the street he could hear her father shouting. When he opened the door, Juan Quintana sent Amadeo packing: 'You're all we need. Get out.' And Amadeo the Idiot went away, head bowed, furious, and cursing under his breath: 'Th-th-that Jo-Jo-Jo-Jonas, son of a b-b-b-bitch.' And he couldn't stop thinking about Berta La Larga's tearful eyes looking at that son of a b-b-b-bitch.

Even though Berta swore she wasn't going out with Jonas, Juan Quintana no longer believed her. When he closed the tavern, he went straight to the lover's tree to search for his daughter's name. At first, he couldn't find it and felt greatly relieved. But it suddenly occurred to him that they were both very tall and maybe her name was higher up, and then he saw it: Jonas and Berta. 'Why didn't I think of looking further up the trunk before.' In a fury he kicked the tree, not that it was to blame, and he ripped off the bark to obliterate the two names – he was in such a frenzy that he made his hands bleed.

By the time he got back to the house, Berta was in bed. He went up to her room still furious and started slapping her, the blood on his hands staining the sheet. Roberta Anaya try to calm him down, but he whacked her too. It was the first time he'd hit his wife: you shouldn't lie to your husband. And Berta La Larga was crushed and Roberta was crushed, and Juan Quintana made the child swear she'd never see Jonas again: 'I swear.' And he left the house, slamming the door behind him, and went down to the tavern to have a whisky: he'd never needed one so badly. And he cried: 'I've lost my daughter.' And he regretted hitting her: 'She's just a child.' On the other hand, he wasn't sorry he'd hit his wife: you shouldn't lie to your husband. Juan Quintana felt very lonely, and he went up to great-grandfather's leg and hugged it, finding a little comfort. Poor great-grandfather, losing his leg must have been so painful. And then it occurred to Juan Quintana that there was something worse than losing your leg: losing your daughter.

The daughter cried in her mother's arms: 'Why is life so unfair? I love Jonas so much, what does it matter that he's from Ponsa if he's a good person?' And it started to rain, echoing her sadness; and Roberta Anaya felt hurt too, but now her daughter was more important: 'You can't go on seeing him.' And Berta had to swear to her mother that she'd never see Jonas again. And that night when Berta got into bed, all she could think about was how much she hated her father and how much she loved Jonas, and she was pained, not by the beating, but by her father's attitude. And while her father was still hugging great-grandfather's leg, Berta hugged her pillow and remembered Jonas's legs (she'd just seen them for the first time), and she smiled timidly and thought how fine they were. Then she looked out of the window: at least it had stopped raining, the moon now reigned supreme in the heavens, and its light brought cheer to Berta's face. She stroked the pink ribbon round her wrist, and remembered her promise: 'I've kept my promise, so help me, God. Life's so unfair.'

Amadeo the Idiot couldn't sleep either. He couldn't stop thinking about Berta La Larga, and he covered his ears so he wouldn't have to hear all over again the villagers' comments about the two lovers. 'Th-th-th-at son of a bitch J-J-J-Jonas.' Alberto the Baker heard Amadeo's muttering and gave him a smack around the head for swearing.

Jonas waited until dark to return to Ponsa: 'How embarrassing to be seen looking like this.' But two men caught him: 'What happened to you?' 'Nothing.' At first the two men laughed, because he looked ridiculous, but Jonas had his answer ready: 'I was robbed on my way home.' They didn't believe him though, it was obviously the inhabitants of Navidad, although Jonas denied it over and over again. Then he went home. Meanwhile, the two men ran to tell the whole village what the inhabitants of Navidad had done to the postman.

The following morning, Roberta Anaya woke up feeling sick after the beating she'd received. She vomited several times, ached all over, and had to stay in bed. Juan Quintana felt slightly guilty, but he didn't say so, because you shouldn't lie to your husband. He forbade Berta La Larga to go out, but she needed so see Jonas and told her father she had to go and give Amadeo the Idiot his reading lesson, and by being very insistent she got him to let her go: 'As long as it's Amadeo the Idiot that's all right.'

Berta went to see Amadeo the Idiot, who was pleased to see her, though he was surprised that she'd brought the reading books since they weren't due for a lesson that day. 'You've got to help me, Amadeo, I have to see him.' When Amadeo realized that Berta wanted to see that son of a bitch Jonas, he flatly refused. But Berta put her arms round him: 'Remember, you're my brother, and brothers help their sisters. Please help me, I can't live without him. Walk to the edge of the village with me, we'll pretend we're going to do reading practice.' Amadeo the Idiot, who couldn't say no to Berta, especially when he saw her eyes full of tears, said he'd help her, and Berta kissed him: 'Thanks, you're the best friend I have.' When they came to the edge of the village, they hid behind some bushes. Berta made Amadeo the Idiot sit down on a huge stone and told him to wait for her there and, just in case, she looked round to make sure he wasn't following her as she walked away. And Amadeo the Idiot cried quietly, and stroked his cheek where Berta had kissed him.

When Berta got to the Corner of Heaven, Jonas wasn't there. She thought maybe she'd never see him again, but he appeared a few moments later, and they fell into a wonderful embrace – nobody in the world could stand in the way of their love. From then on the love between them grew even stronger, if that was possible; the more impossible the love, the more beautiful. After the events of the previous day, Jonas's whole body ached; the animal inside him didn't stir, and he was happy just to have her comfort him with childlike, feminine caresses. That day they communicated only with caresses, and they knew they had to do something if they were to stay together. Berta was miserable as she knew she had to choose between her family and Jonas: 'My poor father.' She loved him in spite of everything. 'If I leave, it'll kill him. And my poor mother.'

Amadeo the Idiot waited for an hour which seemed to go on and on for ever, but he had time enough to decide that he'd never ever help Berta again to come and meet that s-s-s-son of a bitch from Ponsa. After the lovers parted, Berta found Amadeo the Idiot where she'd left him. She kissed him on the forehead and thanked him for his help, then she told him he was the best brother in the world, and the two of them walked back to the village. Berta made him swear not to tell anyone, and she convinced him to come with her again over the following days.

When he got home, Amadeo the Idiot started banging his head against the wall for being such an idiot. He didn't want to be Berta's brother, and he was furious with himself. 'That s-s-s-son of a bitch J-J-Jonas.' He shouted and banged so loud that Remedios had to call Alberto: 'The boy's going to crack his head open.' Even after he had banged his head against the wall so many times, his father gave Amadeo several more whacks about the head: a couple to calm him down, and another couple for swearing.

That night Berta La Larga glanced sadly at her parents, as if she was going to lose them, and she wanted to hug them but didn't. Her mother was still in bed, aching all over after the beating. Berta didn't even get to kiss her mother good night because her selfish father, instead of taking care of Roberta Anaya, grabbed Berta again and interrogated her about the postman and threatened to kill him if he ever saw them together again. Berta locked herself in her room: 'Why is life so unfair?'

Juan Quintana decided to call the doctor. Roberta Anaya had been ill for three days, and she felt worse with each passing hour. He didn't want to call the doctor from Ponsa: the situation being as it was with the neighbouring village, it wouldn't have been appropriate. So he decided to fetch one from Catapalos, the nearest village after Ponsa. The doctor examined Roberta for almost an hour, while Juan Quintana waited impatiently, fearing it was all because of the beating he'd given her.

When the doctor told him, Juan Quintana fell silent. He couldn't believe it. Roberta Anaya was pregnant. He'd lost all hope by now, especially as Roberta Anaya was thirty-eight years old. For a moment, he didn't seem to react at all: he looked so serious that Roberta thought he was appalled by the idea. On the contrary, Juan Quintana was ecstatic: another child! He hugged her, and cried with emotion, he was going to be a father again. He looked tenderly at Roberta Anaya: he'd have to take great care of her during the pregnancy. He'd make sure she didn't eat any yeast, so that the baby didn't turn out so long, and he was sure it would be a boy, and he'd name him after himself, Juan Quintana, and the family name would be passed on. 'Don't tire yourself out, Roberta, you must rest, I'll take care of everything.' He kissed her and felt so happy he even apologized for hitting her:' But promise me you'll always tell me the truth, you shouldn't lie to your husband.'

He wanted the whole world to know that he, Juan Quintana, was going to be a father again. He was the happiest man in the world. He'd always believed that happiness was a delusion, but now he knew he'd been wrong. And, who knows, maybe after the child they were now expecting, they could have more, the army of children he'd always dreamed of, at last, even if he did have to give up Roberta's left breast. He forgot all his problems with the hotel, and forgot Ponsa, and forgot about how upset he was with his daughter. He even forgot Jonas, and before going out to announce the good news, he went to the tavern porch and kissed great-grandfather's leg and said to him: 'I love you, and I'm going to give you a great-great-grandchild, and it's going to be a boy.' He started shouting that Roberta was pregnant, over and over again. People congratulated him, they knew how thrilled he was, but they couldn't show much enthusiasm, because they were very worried by the ever-declining number of tourists.

The men had had a meeting outside the church and decided that three of them, on behalf of all the villagers, would go to the Blue Village to deliver their grievances. The most radical villagers, like Alberto the Baker, were all for declaring war on Ponsa, but the mayor said that fighting was in nobody's interest and first they should try to sort things out amicably. When they asked Juan Quintana, he said all he could think about at the moment was the child who would carry on his name. Joseph the Carpenter was amongst the group of men, and Juan Quintana was in such a good mood that he almost made it up with him, and forgave him, and hugged him – he was his best friend after all – but in the end he didn't do anything, Joseph the Carpenter had behaved very badly, and once again pride got the better of Juan Quintana.

Juan Quintana went to share his happiness with Berta La Larga. He would also tell her that, even if there were to be other children, he loved her more than anything in the world. Roberta Anaya said she'd gone to give Amadeo the Idiot his lesson. 'I have to find her.' He went to the bakery, and Remedios said lately they'd been having lessons in the forest. Juan Quintana thought of going to look for her there but, luckily for Berta, he decided to go back home, he didn't want to leave Roberta on her own: 'I have to take care of her.'

As they had done for the past week, Amadeo the Idiot and Berta La Larga headed for the outskirts of the village. Berta told him to wait for her and he pretended to do as he was told. She was usually away about an hour, which was how long a lesson lasted, and they then returned to the village together, and Berta hurried home so as not to arouse suspicion. That hour seemed endless to Amadeo the Idiot, because you didn't need to be too clever to guess that the two lovers were kissing, embracing. 'D-d-d-damn that s-s-s-son of a bitch Jonas.' He had to do something. And that day he decided to follow Berta into the forest.

In the Corner of Heaven, Jonas and Berta were planning their escape, they had no choice. They didn't care where they went, as long as they were together and, who knows, maybe they could travel, visit all the countries Berta had seen on the stamps, and start a new life: they knew it wouldn't be easy but they'd manage. Jonas would work day and night, he'd do any-thing, so that Berta should want for nothing. 'And when you're eighteen we'll get married.' The idea of running away with him frightened Berta. She remembered what her mother had always told her about men, and she stroked the pink ribbon on her wrist, and she made him swear he wouldn't make love to her until they were married, so as to keep the promise. He agreed, nothing mattered as long as they were together. Berta was proud of Jonas, he loved her so much, but still she couldn't stop thinking about her parents: 'I'm their only child.' And when she looked up at the sky, which had been cloudy for days, she thought she saw a cloud in the shape of a face and it reminded her very much of her father, who she still loved in spite of everything. But he was forcing her to leave the village, so she hated him too. He'd shown he didn't care about her happiness, her father was selfish, and Berta let Jonas kiss her and for a few moments she forgot the promise. She needed him to comfort her, to kiss her. Jonas made the most of Berta's moment of weakness and kissed her passion-ately, and although he did remember the promise, he didn't say anything, especially when he felt her breasts and his hand crept between her legs. It was wonderful.

That day, hidden behind some bushes, Amadeo the Idiot saw them. He couldn't bear to see his beloved Berta embracing that son of a bitch from Ponsa. But above all he couldn't bear to see Jonas touching her. He vented all his fury by banging his head against a tree – not that the tree was to blame – and he did so with such a rage that the whole trunk shook. When Jonas and Berta heard noises, they were frightened and thought they'd been discovered: 'Let's get out of here.' But it was too late. Amadeo the Furious flung himself at Jonas, he wanted to kill him. Frightened, Berta tried to pull them apart and she begged Amadeo the Idiot: 'Stop, please don't hurt him.'

And all the shouting could be heard from the road.

The three villagers on their way back now from Ponsa heard the commotion coming from the forest – they had talked to the Ponsan authorities who had treated them like dirt, telling them they would do exactly as they pleased. They ran to the Corner of Heaven, as somebody was evidently having a fight. Berta begged them to pull the two young men apart. At first they hesitated, because Jonas was a Ponsan, but it was obvious that in his present state Amadeo the Idiot was capable of anything. The postman was on the ground and Amadeo the Idiot was sitting on top of him, about to strangle him. The three men managed to overpower Amadeo the Idiot who was stammering like never before, but it was clear enough that he was saying he was going to kill him, and to calm him down they said justice would be done, and they grabbed Jonas: 'We're going to give you what you deserve.' Berta screamed, shouted, implored. 'Please leave him alone, he hasn't done anything to you.' And the three men dragged Jonas off towards the village. Amadeo the Idiot looked into Berta's eyes seeking under- standing, but he found only hatred, and it saddened him deeply, and now Berta was hitting him and shouting: 'I hate you, I hate you.'

They came to the main street, while the sky began to fill with clouds, and Berta followed them in tears. All the villagers were outraged when they saw the postman again, and they wanted to beat him up to show the neighbouring village that their threats were serious. To make matters worse, it started raining. Berta kneeled on the ground, pleading for mercy, and looked at her father. But Juan Quintana appeared deaf, impervious to his daughter's pleas. Not only that, he wanted to prove to everyone how strong he was, so he joined the calls for revenge.

Amadeo the Idiot couldn't bear to see Berta cry. He locked himself inside the tavern, and had a whisky while covering his ears to block out her screams, but in his heart he could still hear Berta shouting 'I hate you, I hate you', over and over again. He felt like Judas, who betrayed Jesus, and he had another whisky, because only alcohol could ease his pain.

Father Federico tried to calm his parishioners, but it wasn't humanly possible. Roberta Anaya went to her daughter, who was still kneeling in front of her father, and helped her up. In despair, Berta clung to her mother, and just then somebody struck Jonas in his side, and the postman fell to the ground with a cry of pain. And they kicked him, as if he were a murderer, and pelted him with stones, and spat at him, while Berta wept inconsolably, screaming at her father to do something, for the love of God. But Juan Quintana did nothing and they went on kicking poor Jonas, his face now covered in blood. Berta went to Jonas and put her arms round him, kissing him passionately on the mouth to show how strong her love was. For a few moments the entire village fell silent and Berta, a woman in love, again begged for mercy, and her lips, smeared with blood, were a deep red, painfully beautiful to behold.

Emboldened by the alcohol, Amadeo the Idiot came back out: he was seized with an inhuman rage when he saw Berta kiss Jonas, and this time he couldn't stop himself, he grabbed great-grandfather's leg and went for Jonas, his eyes flashing, his arms flailing uncontrollably, his heart wild. Seeing Amadeo the Idiot heading towards the lovers holding great-grandfather's pink leg, Juan Quintana guessed his intentions and, fearing that he'd strike his daughter, he tried to pull her away from Jonas.

Then Amadeo the Idiot raised the leg aloft in both hands, but instead of striking Jonas, he struck Juan Quintana, who was trying in vain to pull Berta away from her beloved. And Juan Quintana collapsed on the ground, his head surrounded by a halo of blood.

There was a deathly hush. Mother and daughter clung to

Juan Quintana's now lifeless body. Berta froze, and a draught of polar air blew through the village. For a few moments the raindrops turned into snow flakes. Jonas no longer felt pain from his wounds; he closed his eyes thinking it was all a bad dream, but then he felt blows to his body, and it was Roberta Anaya, and she screamed at him to leave: 'And don't ever come back.' Jonas couldn't even feel his bleeding body but, making a supreme effort, he struggled to his feet, and stumbled away, and nobody dared say anything to him.

And Juan Quintana, may he rest in peace – he must have needed a rest after all the bustle of the last few days. Berta wouldn't let go of him; they had to wrench her away. Joseph the Carpenter put his arms around her and she felt as cold as a block of ice, she was like a statue, inert, she didn't even have tears in her eyes.

Meanwhile, Amadeo the Idiot disappeared from the village without anyone noticing. Everybody was staring at his parents: Remedios, motionless, still hadn't reacted, and Alberto, when he felt he was being watched, shouted and swore he'd kill his son. Remedios started crying and Alberto, who seemed such a hard man, also began to cry, and the two clung to each other in this vale of tears.

It was snowing for the first time ever in Navidad, and in the whole region, though no-one was in a fit state to notice. At last, Navidad was living up to its name. Under different circumstances, the snow would have become the general topic of conversation, but with a corpse lying there, nobody paid it the slightest attention. Some of the children noticed it with surprise and joy, but they were silenced by their parents. And though it snowed only for a few moments, it stayed incredibly cold for the next few days.

Before he entered his village, Jonas summoned his remaining strength and washed his wounds, but he could do little to disguise the blows to his body, his bruised face, his swollen lips, and when he reached Ponsa he couldn't stop them seeing him. He had already prepared an explanation: 'I was attacked by a wolf.' But they didn't believe him, because there weren't any wolves in the area, and they realized that what had happened was, once again, something to do with Navidad. They bombarded him with so many questions that, to get them to leave him alone, he admitted that he had been to the neighbouring village, but he insisted he was the one to blame, and at last, when he got back home, he fell into Aunt Enriqueta's arms. Poor Jonas needed to unburden himself on somebody and, crying like a baby, he told her everything that had happened, and his aunt was livid with the villagers of Navidad. After cleaning his wounds and making him go to bed, Aunt Enriqueta left the house, determined to tell everyone, even though she'd promised not to say anything. Damn those sons of bitches in Navidad.

That night, the men and women of Navidad mourned the death of Juan Quintana, and just when he felt so happy about the pregnancy too. The only people not weeping were in fact the mother-to-be and Berta La Larga, who was struck dumb. Her brain had gone blank, she couldn't even think about Jonas. Roberta Anaya too sat motionless next to the wooden coffin, keeping all her pain inside. And Joseph the Carpenter felt bereft, his best friend was gone for ever and they hadn't made it up, so he didn't charge the widow for the coffin, it was the least he could do. And he decided it would be an oak coffin, which was so expensive nobody could afford to buy it from him. Juan Quintana deserved the best. Joseph the Carpenter went up to him and, speaking to him as one speaks to the living, he asked him to forgive him for building the other hotel and copying him: 'Forgive me.' Pedro the Blind Man also wanted to say goodbye to Juan Quintana, he'd been so nice to him, but he was so upset he forgot to ask someone to tell him exactly where the coffin was, and almost fell into it.

Poor Roberta, she didn't want to go on living, even though they all tried to cheer her up: 'You're carrying a child, you must be strong.' They felt sorry too for Amadeo the Idiot's parents who were really depressed; Remedios took to her bed and would have nothing to do with the outside world and wept while the women tried to convince her that she wasn't to blame for what had happened, but Remedios was saying it had been her own son, and she couldn't stop crying. Alberto the Baker wouldn't talk to anyone. He just started baking – at least if he set to work it would stop him thinking.

Berta too wanted to die, because she found out her mother was pregnant: 'What's to become of us? My poor mother, and my poor father, who's in heaven now.' She remembered her friend Gracia: they must have met, and great-grandfather. And Berta thought that, as she was so tall, it meant she was nearer to her father. Then Berta glanced up at the sky: unbelievably, the clouds disappeared, giving way to a star-spangled firmament. A few stars shone more brightly, depicting Juan Quintana's face. Death's so unfair.

According to his wishes, Juan Quintana was buried with the leg – just in case great-grandfather needed it in heaven – and there were many remarks about it, as it was the cause of his death. Before the coffin was closed, Roberta Anaya asked if she could be alone with Juan Quintana. She leaned over him, unfastened her bra, took out her left breast and offered it to him even though it wasn't a Sunday or a holiday, placing it near his mouth so he could feel it. And it seemed to Roberta as if Juan Quintana was sucking her breast, because something made her shudder inside, and from that time on her breasts seemed smaller. Somebody even claimed that her left breast had disappeared, but it couldn't be proved as nobody ever saw her naked.

Roberta Anaya wore black for the funeral, and some of the villagers trembled at the thought that the promise was being broken. Although they tried to tell her that she could wear black in her heart, she refused to wear pink and nobody dared contradict her, as she seemed slightly unhinged and not at all receptive to explanations. She started shouting that it was the village's damned promise that was responsible for everything. 'How could you say such a thing about our Pink Virgin.'

Juan Quintana's burial was very moving and painful: in his homily, Father Federico spoke of Juan Quintana as a good and just man, who'd done so much for the village of Navidad with his innovative ideas. Joseph the Carpenter smiled, picturing Juan Quintana revolutionizing heaven: he'd probably give God a tip or two about how to steal customers away from hell. And the church bells were silent, because their ringing would have reminded them of Amadeo the Idiot who, incidentally, still hadn't surfaced.

As they were heading for the cemetery, Alberto the Baker appeared, pitiful, despondent and covered in flour, because he'd been making cakes all night. He kneeled before Roberta Anaya and begged for her forgiveness: 'If only he'd killed me.' The sight of that unsociable, haughty, grumpy man kneeling, was enough to move anyone. Father Federico went over and helped him up and told him to go home to Remedios, who ought not to be on her own.

While Juan Quintana's funeral was being held, the Ponsans gathered together, infuriated by what they'd heard from Jonas's aunt, and decided to block the road and cut Navidad off from the rest of the world. That very same day several men went and cut down half a dozen trees and laid them across the road.

When she got home, Roberta Anaya couldn't bear to look at the walls, chairs, floor; all that she had shared with her husband for so many years. And Berta, who needed her mother's forgiveness, hugged her and swore she'd never leave her. Roberta couldn't even look at her, and when at last she did it was even worse, her eyes were full of hatred. In a fit of madness, her mother started hitting Berta La Larga as hard as she could, accusing her of causing it all, screaming in torment. She woke all the neighbours, who gathered outside the house to see what was going on. Berta tried to calm her mother but it was impossible, and now Roberta Anaya struck out at everything around her, chairs, walls, tables, and screamed at her daughter that she hated her, that because of her she'd lost her husband, her unborn child wouldn't have a father, and to get out, she never wanted to see her ever again.

Weeping, Berta La Larga left the house and then the village, just as it was starting to pour with rain. She wandered about for hours, not knowing where she was going, or what she wanted, or what she was doing in this strange world, until it got dark. She was running away from everything, grief, injustice, anxiety, and now she was walking along the road, and she saw a white horse in the distance and thought she saw Jonas El Largo sitting astride it, coming to rescue her, like in her dream about the tree, and she stood in the middle of the road to attract his attention. Only when the horse was a few yards away did she realize that it was actually a white car, and it almost ran her over.

And so Berta reached Ponsa, exhausted, rain-soaked and grief-stricken. It must have been very late because the streets were deserted, and she was sweating, and her feet were swollen, and her temples were throbbing, and she was in so much pain she could no longer feel it. She made her way to her beloved's house – she knew he lived over the cake shop, and she found it without too much trouble. She banged on the door, shouting Jonas's name. His aunt opened the door in her nightdress and realized this must be the girl Jonas was in love with. Berta almost couldn't speak. She asked breathlessly for Jonas. Aunt Enriqueta stood staring at her speechless, and Berta came past her into the house, and as it wasn't a very big house, she found him straight away. Jonas was in his small bedroom and they embraced: grief and love intertwined just like their bodies. Berta told him to take her to the Cave of the Whale, and Jonas looked at her in surprise, and she said again she wanted to go to the Cave of the Whale.

The two lovers left the house hand in hand; his aunt shouted at Jonas not to go, but the two of them headed for the mountains, in the night, and climbed the crags, and when they arrived Berta saw that the entrance really did look like the mouth of a whale. They fell into a long embrace, so full of desire that, that night, neither Jonas nor Berta could control the animal inside them and they undressed, and they wrapped their bodies round each other and they kissed, and Berta got goose pimples when she felt his skin and they made love to each other and Berta moaned, not just with pleasure, but with rage, and she panted like an animal, and it echoed throughout the cave together with her words of love: 'I love you, I love you, more, more, hold me, hold me.' Jonas had always wanted to travel, and when he saw her naked body, he discovered a whole new world; he travelled thousands of miles across that wonderful human landscape. And he caressed her, going from north to south, from east to west, and he also crossed a sea of skin, and climbed the slope of her breasts until he reached the summit and he entered the jungle of her hair, and his pleasure was so intense that he went round the world several times and got to the moon and saw the stars. Jonas felt he was the most manly of men, and Berta the happiest and unhappiest of women because she couldn't stop thinking about her father. Her brain switched from happiness to the deepest sadness in a split second, her body went from cold to hot, and it was a miracle that her brain didn't short-circuit because she felt as if it was going to explode.

That night, the sky was lit by lightning, then suddenly all the stars came out and it became hot, then it clouded over again, and there were loud rumbles of thunder, and it became cold, and back to hot again. The inhabitants of Ponsa and Navidad looked up at the sky in astonishment, it was the biggest fireworks display the world had ever seen. For a few moments they forgot all their troubles. Even Pedro the Blind Man was astonished, as the thunder was unbelievably loud, and it seemed as if the sky was about to shatter. Joseph the Carpenter remarked that perhaps the extraordinary phenomenon was due to Doña Lucia singing up in heaven and, as was to be expected, it had made God and all the saints really furious, and if she carried on they'd send her straight to hell.

The lovers made love over and over again until dawn. Jonas had waited so long to possess her, he wanted to make up for lost time, and he kissed her so many times that you'd have needed a calculator to add up the number of times, and again, their words of love echoed throughout the cave: 'I love you, I love you.'

And while Jonas El Largo and Berta La Larga made love in the Cave of the Whale, in Navidad they were preparing to make war.

When the villagers of Navidad found out that the Ponsans had blocked the road, they decided to take action. The entire village gathered outside the mayor Feliciano's house and started shouting that they wanted revenge. Even Dolores the Grocer, who was such a calm woman, was very agitated and said she'd go and fight too. All the women joined their voices to hers, and even the children wanted to go to war. 'Be quiet, children, this isn't a game.' And Father Federico looked up to heaven: 'If God doesn't do something soon, this is going to end badly.' And they all remembered Juan Quintana's death; although Amadeo the Idiot was the actual perpetrator, the real culprit was the entire village of Ponsa. The mayor Feliciano, spurred on by his neighbours' calls for vengeance, said the time had come. And during the meeting, which barely lasted ten minutes, it rained three times, the sun came out three times, and it was hot and then cold. The changes in temperature were so dramatic that, inevitably, all the thermometers in Navidad cracked, and Federico the donkey didn't turn a hair.

The men of Navidad went to Ponsa armed with sticks, hoes, pitchforks and scythes. Joseph the Carpenter made his own weapon out of a strip of wood attached to a handle. Behind them came the women carrying kitchen utensils such as frying pans, mortars, brooms, saucepans and meat tenderizers. At the last minute, Margarita Cifuentes, who hadn't left her house since she separated from her husband, joined the group, to everyone's surprise, particularly the mayor Feliciano's. He went up to her and thanked her for her support. Margarita Cifuentes nodded – luckily for everyone she still wasn't speaking. Most of the villagers heading off to do battle had terrible colds, in fact with so many changes in temperature it was a mercy they hadn't all fallen ill. Only the old folk stayed behind, and the children, who were still screaming because they wanted to go and fight, and again they had to have it explained to them that this was no game, and Father Federico was appointed their guardian, so now he was father to forty children.

Federico the donkey started braying; it was the first time in his life he'd predicted the approach of a terrible storm, even though this was a human one; the way things were going, but for a miracle, the donkey was going to get it right.

The villagers were nearing Ponsa, shouting – between sneezes – demanding justice and chanting in unison: 'The only good Ponsan is a dead one.' They became even more enraged when they saw the blocked road for themselves, with several trees lying across it so that only small vehicles such as motorbikes and bicycles could get through. But what really incensed them was seeing the village painted blue. They'd copied everything, right down to placing a sign at the edge of the village which read: 'Please respect the manner of dress of the inhabitants of Ponsa.'

They came to the main street shouting 'murderers', and the Ponsans, realizing that the villagers were in deadly earnest, hid inside their houses. Now the cry went up: 'Cowards, you're all cowards.' And as there was no-one to fight, the inhabitants of Navidad destroyed shop windows, the fountain in the square, benches, porches and anything else they saw around them. At which point, the Ponsans responded, at first hurling insults and then coming out into the street: the men first, and the women behind them when they saw that the female population of Navidad was also prepared to fight. Some tourists who were visiting Ponsa thought they were witnessing some sort of theatre performance organized by the two villages, but when they got closer and saw the looks of hatred, they realized that the best thing they could do was get out of there.

And so the war between the two villages began, and if there wasn't a massacre it was because both sides were too poor to own any firearms. It was named the battle of the two colours – as if it were a game of chess, but in this case with pink pieces and blue pieces. Somebody even claimed to have seen a pink dog fighting a blue dog, but that was actually impossible as we already know that the only pink dog in Navidad came to a sticky end.

Everyone fought as best he could – including the women who fought each other. Several of them had clumps of hair pulled out and, incidentally, more than one of them was found to be wearing a wig. They scratched one another with their nails, tore one another's dresses, walloped one another with pans and brooms. Dolores the Grocer was one of the most effective: she charged at the men and, making the most of her short stature, whacked them in their most delicate parts with a meat tenderizer, and they writhed in pain, while she smiled with satisfaction.

Even Pedro the Blind Man took part, striking out blindly – literally – and he clobbered anything within reach with his stick, sometimes he missed and sometimes he didn't, and he walloped people on his own side as well. Joseph the Carpenter's sword snapped on the first head it struck, proving, as Juan Quintana had said, that he used very poor quality wood. As for the Montalbo brothers, thanks to the war, they were as close as ever again, and while one of them charged at the enemy, the other one covered him.

The children of Ponsa were luckier than the children of Navidad, because they were allowed to fight, even if only from the balconies of their houses. They had a grand time throwing apples, marbles, potatoes, buckets of water, eggs, pears and anything else they could lay their hands on at the villagers of Navidad and, making the most of the situation, the crafty ones threw their school books too. As they were rather high up, sometimes they hit their targets and sometimes they missed.

There were many wounded from blows with sticks, kitchen utensils, brooms, frying pans. Others were more seriously wounded, particularly some of the men who were stabbed or struck hard on the head. The mayor Feliciano was one of those who came off worst: someone stuck a knife in his back which only narrowly missed his heart. Margarita Cifuentes saved his life because she saw that a man was about to attack him and she recovered the power of speech just in time to shout his name: 'Feliciano, watch out.' Thanks to her, the mayor moved out of the way and the knife only struck him in the shoulder.

Gradually, the Ponsans gained the upper hand. They were fighting on their own turf so they could entrench themselves in their houses, and they weren't as exhausted as their opponents, who'd hardly slept a wink since Juan Quintana's death.

The battle could be heard from the Cave of the Whale.

Startled, Jonas and Berta came out of their hiding place to see what was going on. They hid behind a rocky outcrop, from where they could see the two villages doing battle. Berta was stunned, she couldn't believe her eyes. She felt she was to blame for the war, for her father's death, for her mother's unhappiness. The sky filled with such dark clouds that it seemed like night-time. Jonas saw how sad she was and hugged her with all his might. He covered her eyes so she couldn't see the absurd war and the two of them headed back inside the Cave of the Whale.

Meanwhile, in Navidad, oblivious to everything, Alberto the Baker had made so many cakes that he'd used up all his ingredients, and Remedios was still crying, only getting out of bed to go and spend a penny. Roberta Anaya also remained shut up in her house; her grief-stricken moans could be heard from the street. Father Federico would have liked to go to see her but, with forty children to look after, he couldn't manage it, he didn't even have time to pray for those who'd gone to war. The old ladies were praying though, their contribution to the battle was praying to the Virgin that she restore peace. But, to their surprise, they saw that someone had divested the Pink Virgin of her clothes. And when they came out of the church they stared perplexed at the sky which was as black as coal. Without doubt, it was a punishment from God.

The sky must have been very black indeed because the two villages stopped fighting for a few moments and stared at it. Joseph the Carpenter felt a drop land under his eye, like a tear. And the same happened to the mayor Feliciano and to Margarita Cifuentes and to all of them: a tear from heaven settled on their faces, and they looked as if they'd all agreed to start crying.

In the Cave of the Whale, Berta started shedding tears once

again, and she did so at such a rate that they merged to form a river of tears. Jonas tried to comfort her, but his caresses, his embraces, his words echoing round the cave were no use: 'I love you, I love you.'

And now, the two sets of villagers fought in the rain. The inhabitants of Navidad were closer to defeat than ever, but just when it seemed that all was lost, Amadeo the Idiot appeared. They were surprised to see him, but they greeted him warmly. When all was said and done, he was one of them, and he started fighting like a lunatic against all the Ponsans. But it was raining so hard that they couldn't see a thing. It was impossible to go on fighting. The ground was so slippery they could barely stand up. Some Ponsans took refuge in their houses, and the villagers of Navidad also decided to withdraw, all except Amadeo the Idiot, who seemed not to care about the rain and went on striking out to left and right. He was now the only one still fighting the Ponsans, and Joseph the Carpenter shouted at him to stop and come back with them. Amadeo the Idiot, distracted for a moment by his shouting, was stabbed in the heart, and he fell to the ground. 'He's dead.' And on his face appeared the smile that vanished the day he killed Juan Quintana. The rain beat down on his bleeding body and it turned red, forming such a huge pool of blood around him that you would have thought an ox had bled to death. Amadeo the Idiot's eyes were open and the rain flowing over them looked like a thousand tears.

The villagers returned in silence to Navidad – all except for Margarita Cifuentes who was helping the mayor along; he was very weak as a result of his injury. Once again she was talking nineteen to the dozen: 'Don't you worry Feliciano, I'll take care of you and you'll get better, you've been luckier than poor Amadeo, God rest his soul, blah, blah, blah.'

Berta wept as never before. Jonas, saddened by her crying

and by the war was also amazed. He couldn't understand how Berta could cry so much. Her tears would have filled several buckets. Lucky for humanity that Berta didn't witness Amadeo the Idiot's death: she was so fond of him, there would have been a second Flood.

Without mercy, rain flooded everything once more. Streets first, then ground floors, and the two villages now had to fight to save their possessions. Once again the inhabitants of Navidad had to fill up and empty buckets but, after the battle, any villagers not wounded were exhausted and their colds were worse, and their superhuman efforts were futile because it was raining much harder than before they made the promise. And while he bailed out water, Joseph the Carpenter mused that Doña Lucia must be to blame, she must still be singing, in hell now, and he bet that Beelzebub had got really angry and was getting his revenge: 'If she goes on singing, they'll send her back up to heaven, and at this rate it'll go on for ever.' And the wind began to blow furiously, joining forces with the rain, and devastated everything. The church clock broke down again and, by chance, it stopped at exactly ten past seven, like before it was mended.

After several weeks of rain, the inhabitants of Navidad had no choice but to abandon their village, taking refuge high in the mountains. A few refused to leave their houses, amongst them Alberto the Baker and his wife Remedios, who had lost the will to live, and it was no use the whole village telling them that their son Amadeo the Idiot died like a hero. Alberto the Baker handed over all the cakes he'd made so they'd have provisions. And when they all left, he got into bed with Remedios, and they put their arms around each other, and that's how they must have died.

Father Federico tried to convince Roberta Anaya to leave

Navidad. He said she had to think of her unborn child, but she wanted to stay with Juan Quintana. But Joseph the Carpenter couldn't allow his best friend's wife to drown, so he picked her up and forced her to come with him.

Without so much as a by-your-leave, water ran into every corner: into wardrobes, soaking all the pink clothes, and making the colour run; into the painting room at Joseph the Carpenter's workshop, mixing with the cans of pink paint; and when it entered Berta La Larga's room, it washed away her love letters as well as the stamps Jonas had given her: France, Canada, Egypt and the whole world now travelled too, floating away on the water. The Pink Pirate tavern looked like a boat that had sunk to the bottom of the sea, and so did the hotel, and when water flowed into the restaurant it mixed with all the pink food colouring.

The houses gradually returned to their original colour, as an infinity of pink droplets slid down their walls, until they all inevitably collapsed. The last building standing was the church, but it too succumbed in the end: the bells rang for one last time as they collapsed along with the bell tower, and crashed down on top of the clock mechanism which, surprisingly, started working for a few minutes, before stopping for ever.

The Pink Virgin, who'd lost her pink clothes, was abducted by the swelling waters and swept away on the current: only her head bobbed up above the water, and she looked as if she'd been shipwrecked, and her eyes were sad. The lovers' tree, which wasn't to blame for anything, drifted away, and with it went the love stories of so many generations.

The entire village was submerged by the water, which swept away everything in its path: pink cars, pink tables, pink chairs, pink lamps, pink rugs, pink towels, pink beds, pink toys, pink walls, pink clothes, pink kitchen utensils, pink motorbikes and bicycles. From the sky, it looked like a vast river of pink water flowing at great speed.

And the same happened in the village of Ponsa. The Ponsans had to abandon their homes and take refuge high up in the mountains. The water turned blue, and swept away blue cars, blue walls, blue clothes, blue kitchen utensils, blue motorbikes and bicycles.

A great torrent of blue water flowed furiously out of the village, until it came to the road block. The trees lying across the road acted as a dam, stopping the water. But such pressure built up that the trees gave way and the water, in all its fury, surged on.

And so the great river of pink water flowing from Navidad and the river of blue water flowing from Ponsa merged, gradually producing another colour.

A plane flying over the area informed air traffic control that it could make out a huge purplish stain.

EPILOGUE

Even today meteorologists still can't explain the torrential rains over Navidad and Ponsa. Not just because of the enormous quantity of rain that fell, but because, unbelievably, the sky remained totally clear in the rest of the region. The abrupt changes in temperature during the days leading up to the so-called Purple Flood are also a mystery. Particularly in Navidad, where snow caused it to live up to its name for the first time.

The inhabitants of Navidad, of course, were convinced that it all happened because they broke the promise and because they went to war, and they were sure the Pink Virgin had been displeased. A very unscientific explanation, but it was the most convincing anyone ever came up with.

The two villages disappeared for ever and their inhabitants had to make new lives for themselves. Some decided to move to the capital, while others settled in nearby villages.

The mayor Feliciano and Margarita Cifuentes made it up and were amongst those who went to live in the capital. Feliciano had no choice: she'd saved his life so it was the least he could do, and sometimes he thinks maybe it would have been better if he'd died, because Margarita Cifuentes chatters away nineteen to the dozen once more, and he's fed up with listening to her tell everyone how she saved his life. But he still sees the young woman he met in Navidad, in secret, and his visits to her provide his only moments of peace. He knows almost nothing about her because he doesn't let her speak.

Pedro the Blind Man moved to the capital too. He tries to make a living from begging, but there's stiff competition. Lots of others do the same: blind people, paralysed people, amputees, young children. On more than one occasion he's had problems with the authorities who've accused him of being a flasher, because with all those women around he just gets carried away, and he always has his flies undone.

As we've already mentioned, the Montalbo brothers were reconciled as a result of the war. They set up their own theatre company, and for several years now they've toured the country with a play about the tragic story of the Pink Village, to great acclaim. The high point of the show is the love story between Jonas El Largo and Berta La Larga, played by two puppets. In the final act they explain that the lovers, being so tall, were swept away by the strong wind that blew during the Purple Flood and that they disappeared for ever.

Joseph the Carpenter moved to a village near Navidad and opened a new workshop. He helped Roberta Anaya to get on and, if it hadn't been for him, she would almost certainly have died. Roberta Anaya gave birth to a daughter and not a son as Juan Quintana had wanted, but that's life. And in gratitude to Joseph the Carpenter, she decided to call her Gracia. Although still very young, Gracia already shows signs of having as vivid an imagination as her father. At only seven years of age, she makes her own toys with old bits of wood that Joseph the Carpenter gives her. He's delighted with little Gracia and treats her like a daughter.

Father Federico was posted to a village in the north of the country. Old Inés went with him, and she keeps house for him. The priest really misses his former parishioners, as he'd become very fond of them. He even misses Margarita Cifuentes, who kept him informed of everything that was going on. In spite of everything, she wasn't a bad person.

Surprisingly, Federico the donkey survived too. Nobody knows how, nor exactly when, but he appeared months later on the outskirts of the village of Catapalos. Thanks to the rain he's returned to his original grey colour and he neither brays nor shakes his ears, nothing. When a human being goes near him, he runs off.

Dolores came off best. She went to live with her only sister in the capital. She felt lonely and directionless. Perhaps the immensity of the city overwhelmed her more than the others because of her short stature. She fell into such a deep depression that she had to be put in a psychiatric hospital. There, she fell in love with one of the other patients who had lost his spouse, like her, and was suffering from depression as a result. They were married a year later. Best of all, Dolores was, unbelievably, taller than him. Understandable really, because her intended was a dwarf. His name was Gustavo and he worked in a travelling circus. His wife had been a dwarf like him and he'd loved her very much. His eyes were as blue as the sky. When he found out that Dolores was from Navidad he asked her about a little girl he met there who was very tall. Dolores realized he meant Berta La Larga.

Many believed that Berta and Jonas, being so tall, had been blown away by the wind, but the truth was very different: they managed to escape together and settled in a village near the capital. The early days were hard. Jonas had to do all kinds of work and they still only just had enough to eat. On the day of Berta La Larga's eighteenth birthday they got married. The priest was surprised they didn't have engagement rings. They said they did, but that they were in the sky. That day, a cloud appeared in the heavens again shaped like a huge engagement ring.

Berta became pregnant and had a son they named Juan Jonas, after her father and the place where the child was conceived. Juan Jonas is five now and he's almost five feet tall. The other children often make fun of him for being so tall. Berta comforts him tenderly and, remembering her father, she tells him that people who are very tall are lucky because they're closer to heaven.

After Navidad disappeared, nobody ever mentioned the legend of the Rainbow again. But it always rains, wherever Berta La Larga is, on the anniversary of Juan Quintana's death.

Barcelona, Tossa de Mar (Gerona) and the Azores (Portugal)
September 1995 –April 1996

Th-th-th-thank you f-f-f-for reading this b-b-b-book.

AMADEO THE IDIOT

Madam reader: thank you for reading this book. I hope to meet you in person some day, and I'm sure I'll find you very attractive, particularly your . . .

PEDRO THE BLIND MAN

I always said, Navidad was the kind of place you could write pages and pages about, and not just since the promise to the Virgin, but long before; my poor grandmother, for instance, who lived so splendidly in the capital and had the misfortune to fall in love with a man from Navidad, and of course when they got married they went to live in Navidad, she'd always lived like a lady, then suddenly she was the wife of a peasant, because that's what my grandfather was, a peasant, even though he had quite a bit of land, and made a good living, Navidad's just a miserable little village, and it doesn't even have a measly tea room for ladies, and you can't buy a decent dress there, luckily Feliciano's never minded me going to the capital, where a woman like me can find suitable clothes, the boutique Impériale, that's my favourite, the owner's French, and she goes to Paris every year to buy clothes, I'll go to Paris some day, I'm sure, Feliciano's the problem. I'll never persuade him, he says he prefers to work, he's so peculiar, when we got married he hated working, but now I don't know what's up with him, blah, blah.

MARGARITA CIFUENTES

Whatever she says goes.

THE MAYOR FELICIANO

Why the hell should I have to thank the readers, when I end so badly?

ALBERTO THE BAKER

What I most miss about life on Earth is my Roberta's left breast.

JUAN QUINTANA

T for thank you and S for see you soon.

BERTA LA LARGA

APPENDIX 1

The story in numbers:

Number of tears shed by Berta La Larga after her father's death: 106,567.

Number of times Jonas and Berta made love in the Cave of the Whale: 56.

Number of times Amadeo the Idiot banged his head against the wall: 885.

Number of cakes made by Alberto the Baker after his son's death: 995.

Number of Our Fathers said by old Inés after the flood: 7,395.

Number of words said by Margarita Cifuentes after she recovered the power of speech: 85,789,456.

Number of times the donkey brayed throughout the story: 899.

Number of times Juan Quintana sucked Roberta Anaya's left breast up to the time of his death: 1,729.

Appendix 2

Technical features of Roberta Anaya's left breast:

— Total weight: 4½lbs.
— Height: 9¼ inches.
— Diameter: 7 inches.
— Shape: round, very round.
— Taste: very sweet.
— Consistency: firm and smooth.
— Colour: cream.

The 2 times table according to Amadeo the Idiot:

2 x 1 = 1
2 x 2 = 2
2 x 3 = 5
2 x 4 = 12
2 x 5 = 10*
2 x 6 = 26
2 x 7 = 28
2 x 8 = I d-d-d-don't know
2 x 9 = N-n-n-no idea

* Pure fluke.

APPENDIX 4

Countries visited by Berta La Larga thanks to the stamps Jonas gave her:

- — Argentina
- — Canada
- — Egypt
- — United States
- — Spain
- — France
- — Guatemala
- — India
- — Iran
- — Liechtenstein
- — Mexico
- — Portugal
- — Russia

APPENDIX 5

Juan Quintana's cure for insomnia. Counting customers:

1 customer, 2 customers, 3 customers, 4 customers, 5 customers, 6 customers, 7 customers, 8 customers, 9 customers, 10 customers, 11 customers, 12 customers, 13 customers, 14 customers, 15 customers, 16 customers, 17 customers, 18 customers, 19 customers, 20 customers, 21 customers, 22 customers, 22 customers, 23 customers, 24 customers, 25 customers, 26 customers, 27 customers, 28 customers, 29 customers, 30 customers, 31 customers, 32 customers, 33 customers, 34 customers, 35 customers, 36 customers, 37 customers, 38 customers, 39 customers, 40 customers, 41 customers, 42 customers, 43 customers, 44 customers, 45 customers, 46 customers, 47 customers, 48 customers, 49 customers, 50 customers, 51 customers, 52 customers, 53 customers, 54 customers, 55 customers, 56 customers, 57 customers, 58 customers, 59 customers, 60 customers, 61

customers, 62 customers, 63 customers, 64 customers, 65 customers, 66 customers, 67 customers, 68 customers, 69 customers, 70 customers, 71 customers, 72 customers, 73 customers, 74 customers, 75 customers, 76 customers, 77 customers, 78 customers, 79 customers, 80 customers, 81 customers, 82 customers, 83 customers, 84 customers, 85 customers, 86 customers, 87 customers, 88 customers, 89 customers, 90 customers, 91 customers, 92 customers, 93 customers, 94 customers, 95 customers, 96 customers, 97 customers, 98 customers, 99 customers, 100 customers, 101 customers, 102 customers, 103 customers, 104 customers, 105 customers, 106 customers, 107 customers, 108 customers, 109 customers, 110 customers, 111 customers, 112 customers, 113 customers, 114 customers, 115 customers, 116 customers, 117 customers, 118 customers, 119 customers, 120 customers, 121 customers, 122 customers, 123 customers, 124 customers, 125 customers, 126 customers, 127 customers, 128 customers, 129 customers, 130 customers, 131 customers, 132 customers, 133 customers, 134 customers, 135 customers, 136 customers, 137 customers, 138 customers, 139 customers, 140 customers, 141 customers, 142 customers, 143 customers, 144 customers, 145 customers, 146 customers, 147 customers, 148 customers, 149 customers, 150 customers, 151 customers, 152 customers, 153 customers, 154 customers, 155 customers, 156 customers, 157 customers, 158 customers, 159 customers, 160 customers, 161 customers, 162 customers, 163 customers . . . Until you fall asleep.

Insults hurled at Jonas El Largo in Navidad:

Son of a bitch	Rat
Bastard	Jerk
Irresponsible fool	Poof
Yob	Lout
Filthy pig	Blockhead
Simpleton	Retard
Cretin	Degenerate
Stupid idiot	Imbecile
Mental defective	Brute
Dummy	Bonehead
Lunatic	Sod
Thickhead	Nonentity
Swine	Chump
Dope	Dolt
Halfwit	Clumsy Idiot
Moron	Git
Dimwit	Ass
Useless idiot	Berk
Dunce	Judas
Arsehole	Pig

APPENDIX 7

Meteorological phenomena that occurred in Navidad in the hours following Juan Quintana's death:

 Sunny

 Overcast

 Changeable

 Rain

 Cold front

 Storms

 Snow

 Warm front

Number of letters contained in this book:

Number of A's: 26,278
Number of B's: 4,080
Number of C's: 6,304
Number of D's: 8,356
Number of E's: 23,674
Number of F's: 1,007
Number of G's: 1,620
Number of H's: 2,040
Number of I's: 10,890
Number of J's: 1,366
Number of K's: 16
Number of L's: 10,074
Number of M's: 4,491
Number of N's: 11,952
Number of Ñ's: 402
Number of O's: 16,563
Number of P's: 4,629
Number of Q's: 2,852
Number of R's: 12,342
Number of S's: 12,894
Number of T's: 7,652
Number of U's: 8,670
Number of V's: 2,145

Number of W's: 6,075
Number of X's: 125
Number of Y's: 2,522
Number of Z's: 746

Total: 183,696